THE KINSMEN

THE KINSMEN

by

William Haggard

WALKER AND COMPANY
NEW YORK

First published in the United States of America
in 1974 by the Walker Publishing Company, Inc.

ISBN: 0-8027-5308-6

Library of Congress Catalog Card Number: 74-82171

Printed in the United States of America.

10   9   8   7   6   5   4   3   2   1

1

Mike Horan looked round his comfortable room. He was waiting to be beaten up.

The room was a surprising one, or rather would have surprised an innocent who supposed that a man who'd done time in prison would live like a Dickensian criminal or else in a tasteless and flashy luxury. Michael Horan's room was neither of these. His landlady spoke telly American and she sometimes called the room a duplex. In fact it was on a single level but the bed folded neatly away in the wall. A bathroom and a tiny kitchen were unobtrusively and cleverly hidden. Long windows looked out on a Kensington square. There were some good antiques and a parquet floor, a rug or two and a baby grand. Mike Horan played it rather well, but he was a practical man with few illusions. He was a talented amateur and knew it, who would never cross the immense divide between the amateur and the first class professional, and a lifetime spent playing in bars and cafés, for music societies in Midland towns, was something he had never considered. To begin with there was no money in it and Michael had a proper respect, if not for the abstract idea of money, at least for the very real things it would buy. He liked the best, the modest best, and had always been perfectly ready to work for it, though when his great aunt Lilian Gregg died at last he could then afford to loaf a little. He wasn't greedy for all the old lady's wealth but she'd told him that she'd remember him handsomely, and she wouldn't cut him out of her Will simply because he had once been in prison.

Just the once and old Lady Gregg was civilized: in fact before old age had caught her she'd been as tough as a boot and agreeably worldly. Michael had real affection for her quite apart from any hopes of benefit, and he was confident that when she thought of his scrapes she would think of them with a tolerant smile. So she wouldn't do the dirt on him because he'd twice lost his wicked Horan temper.

He caught himself reflecting dourly that his imprisonment had been very bad luck but he suppressed the thought at once as self pity. But he hadn't intended to hurt the man—not the Grievous Bodily Harm rap they'd hung on him. He would have confessed that he'd lost his terrible temper. The man had rushed him swinging his clumsy fists, though Horan hadn't been able to prove it. Mike Horan had been in an odd profession—not criminal, simply not quite respectable —and this director had been quintessential establishment. Horan had had no chance in court. The judge had read him a tedious homily, then sent him to prison to cool his heels. He had done so with an ill-concealed relish; he'd had power to protect the established; he'd used it.

Michael Horan smiled sadly—he'd known something of brawling. He could defend himself when he had to and did. The army had taught him to use his hands, his feet and most of his body too, so why not use them now again when this couple came to beat him up? They always worked in couples. Never more.

He smiled again for it wouldn't be sensible. Like piano-playing he knew his place. He was competent at unarmed combat but he was far below professional standards. Moreover there'd be more than one and probably they'd bring coshes too. Annoy them and maybe break a bone and you'd simply make your beating worse. The best thing was to lie still and take it. The frighteners had already called. A totally unfruitful visit since he hadn't the money to pay his debt. So it wasn't the frighteners now, it was punishment. From the man he'd offended that was inevitable.

It had occurred to him to go to the police but he had turned the idea down at once. 'Police protection' was an often-used phrase but in practice it meant almost nothing. He was comfortably out of his time on probation, which he'd earned by exemplary conduct in prison, but the police would know he'd been in jail and be unlikely to stretch their resources to help him. They'd assume it was something to do with prison, tobacco perhaps or some sodomites' feud. In any case what did the hackneyed words mean? Something, perhaps, for V.I.P.s and something for essential witnesses, but the idea that you could call on the police for round-the-clock protection indefinitely was as absurd as that other he'd thought of first, that he'd simply lock himself in and wait— wait till the heat blew over finally. But he knew very well that it wouldn't blow over, and in fact he couldn't live long mewed up. He had to buy cigarettes and food, the various needs of a bachelor life, and these trips in the streets were very unnerving, much worse than staying at home and waiting. He knew what could happen: they could easily snatch him. . . .

Some field several miles from the nearest village, dragging his broken body for help. Here he had at least a telephone and a doctor he knew would mind his own business. It wouldn't be easy to take but he must.

Nor would his neighbours interfere. His landlady lived in two rooms in the basement and most of the day she worked in an office. At the top of the house was a biggish flat but the old General and his lady wife were both of them as deaf as stones. Across the landing was another single which was kept by a Miss Charlotte Tellier. Michael Horan didn't like her much. To call her a tart would be overstatement, she was what in other, robuster times had been known by the simple word adventuress. Offer her money— she'd slap your face; but take her to dinner a couple of times, suggest a warm week in the South of France, and provided she felt you were good for a present she would come and she would give good value. Mike Horan didn't care much for the type, but nor did he dislike her actively. She had made a routine pass at him but he hadn't resented that. He had laughed. There were thousands of Charlotte Telliers in London. In any case he had need to keep in with her since her mother kept the nursing home where old Lady Gregg was slowly dying. It was a very expensive home indeed.

So if Charlotte heard a struggle next door Charlotte would promptly bolt her door. She wasn't the type to expose her neck. The General then ...

The doorbell rang sharply.

Horan rose with a sigh and opened the door. He didn't bother to use the chain on the door-frame but threw it wide open and stood waiting to take it.

'Is the lady of the house at home?'

'I'm afraid there is none. I live alone.'

The woman flogging cosmetics left.

Michael Horan went back to his chair and sat down. The anticlimax had shaken him badly. It was almost three days since the frighteners' call and their very explicit threat of violence. The tension had been hard to bear and this tiresome woman had cruelly increased it. He would have liked a drink but had finished it yesterday and his trips outside must be kept to a minimum. For the first time he wavered about his neighbours. The General, he thought—slip upstairs or ring him. Tell him part of the truth and ask him to sit with you. The General was into his later seventies but he was a formidable figure still and like many of his age and profession he had probably kept some sort of weapon.

No, he couldn't do that, it wouldn't be decent. Either the old man would earn a coshing or if he used his weapon he'd be in serious trouble. To call him would be grossly improper. He was a game old cock and would certainly come and he wasn't the sort of establishment figure which a man of Horan's background detested. On the contrary he admired him greatly and moreover he was still in his debt.

Horan's father had been a regular soldier and when he had died there'd been little money. Mike Horan had been good at his books but there had still been something called National Service, so he'd turned down his grant and the chance of deferment and signed for three years in the regiment he fancied, not one which recruited much in Glasgow. He was confident he could earn a commission and when he had one he'd make the army his life.

It had certainly changed since his father's time, who had served without going higher than Major. Look at the recruitment adverts .... 'Which of these men is a Colonel?' Which indeed? The answer was the five who looked ordinary, like milkmen or door-to-door salesmen or plumbers. The sixth who looked like a soldier was not. Yes, the army had changed on the surface certainly, but elsewhere it had hardly changed at all. For the moment he'd made the officer squad, which in theory wasn't supposed to exist, there'd been an N.C.O. who had made it his business to make Michael Horan's life a misery. At first he had suffered as best he could, telling himself, though without conviction, that this was part of an old-fashioned system, but he had realized after a couple of months that it was more than that, this drill sergeant hated him. As an Ulsterman he would break this Mick and he succeeded in doing just that. Horan struck him.

The machine had been put in gear at once but the throttle was handled with some discretion. The regiment had been a civilized one and it loathed washing dirty linen in public. There'd been a good deal of private toing and froing between the Major of Mike Horan's company and the Lieutenant Colonel who ran the battalion. Finally, Horan had heard much later, the Regimental Colonel's ear had been sought on an unofficial occasion. He had listened and given the judgement of Solomon: this sergeant was clearly a shocking bully and should be quietly transferred to the sort of regiment where that sort of thing was

10

still accepted. Horan must be severely punished but he shouldn't be sent to the glasshouse and broken. But naturally they couldn't commission him now.

That Regimental Colonel's ear had been the ear of the ageing General upstairs. Horan wondered if he remembered it. Probably. In any case that wasn't relevant. He simply couldn't put him at risk, a decent old boy who'd behaved very decently. There were plenty of his type who would not have.

... I don't think I'm really a violent man, simply one with an over-strong sense of injustice plus a wholly uncontrollable temper. Which were very uncomfortable things to have especially if you lacked the privilege which would have earned them your equals' easy tolerance. God help me, I'm a Celt at heart, though my grandmother Gregg was a lowland Scot.

Mike Horan got up and made strong black coffee. No doubt he'd been foolish to lose all that money, a sudden onrush of the gambler's fever when he wasn't by nature a regular gambler, but he wouldn't submit to a serious savaging. Mike Horan couldn't pay on the nail but he would when old great aunt Lilian died and that couldn't be more than a matter of months. Already she had her very bad days and her doctor had been shaking his head.

Perhaps a mild beating-up was permissible—after all he had bilked at a gambling club and that was a dangerous thing to do—but only if it were done within reason. That he could take, or he hoped he could, but if they started on breaking bones or disfiguring him he'd lose his temper again and make things worse. His hope was that they wouldn't intend to since an injured man in hospital meant inquiries about his injuries, and that they would wish to avoid if they could. But if they overstepped that and Mike Horan fought back ...

In the event they overstepped from the start. When the doorbell rang for the second time and Horan again stood with open door they rushed him at once and clubbed him down. No talk at all, not even threats. They went at him compactly and snarling. One man kicked out as he struggled to rise. He missed his target by the merest inch but he hurt Michael Horan and he frightened him badly. If this was that sort of beating he'd had it.

An all too familiar sensation engulfed him, blind fury at what he considered unjust. They meant to maim him and he hadn't earned that. The two men had backed away and were grinning. One of them said:

'That was only *hors d'oeuvre*.' He had a great deal of hair in front of his ears and mean pig's eyes in a pasty face.

Mike Horan fought himself and lost. If the man hadn't spoken he might have won, have taken his beating as best he might. Instead he rose and chopped him down. His unarmed combat was still quite good. The second man promptly drew a chain. The first got to his feet with his cosh and used it.

Mike Horan, several hours later, was grateful, for the coshing had saved him a good deal of pain. Not that he wasn't feeling it now as he crawled to the telephone, ringing his doctor. His whole body ached in a single bruise and he could see that he had been sick on the floor.

12

The doctor was a personal friend and he went over Horan with care and sympathy. 'No major bones broken but you've certainly taken it. Happily you've no open wounds but you do have quite severe concussion. I ought to send you into hospital now.' He said it as a sort of question; he knew something—not all—of his patient's history.

'Not hospital,' Horan said.

'Let's see.' He was a doctor in an unusual practice and this wasn't the first time an injured man had shied away from hospital treatment. 'Let's see,' he said again. 'Can you walk?'

'I think I could get to the bed if you helped me.'

The doctor released the bed from the wall, then pulled Horan up to his feet. He staggered.

'Steady,' the doctor said as they made it. He was thinking that Horan had answered a question; he had staggered but lucidly answered a question. The concussion might not be as bad as he'd thought. 'I'm giving you something to put you out. I'm running a risk in not calling an ambulance, but then, you see, I don't practise in Harley Street. By the way, can you follow me?'

'Yes I can.'

'Then I'll be back in two hours but I make you no promises. If you're worse I'll have to send you to hospital but if you're holding your own I'll send someone to care for you. Naturally he won't be a doctor, or rather he's not on the Register now, but he knows his business. Just don't ask any questions. And one other thing. Do you drink?'

'A little. But there's nothing here to drink at the moment.'

13

'Excellent. It could easily kill you.'

Mike Horan didn't reply to this. The drug had bitten, he wasn't conscious.

The doctor found the modest bathroom, fetching a basin, an ancient rag. He mopped Mike Horan's vomit carefully. He was a very good doctor, a better friend.

2

Paul Martiny was eating Rex Lucas's luncheon but he was doing so with a certain caution. There were people who considered Lucas a criminal of the very worst kind, the men who believed that anyone who ran gambling clubs at enormous profit was by that act and by that alone a very anti-social creature. Paul Martiny didn't share this view. The people Rex Lucas mostly fleeced were in Paul Martiny's opinion stupid. Either they were degenerates, the possessors of inherited wealth which they hadn't the skills to husband properly, or else they had made a bomb in property, in some business which not so long ago nobody had even heard of, and were gambling as a symbol of status. In either case he wished them ill, and if men like Rex Lucas bled them white there was justice in that if not a court's.

God damn the courts and all their flummeries. Only a few years ago Rex Lucas's name had in fact been Loukas and he was still as Greek as that strong blood came. But he wasn't a proper criminal, or not what Paul Martiny considered so.

Paul Martiny had been born in a world whose advantages he gladly accepted but whose values he had decided were nonsense. He was what was still called a country gentleman since they lived in the country and were deemed to be gentle, and the criminals whose affairs he managed assumed that he did it for lack of money. This was the general opinion. Mistakenly.

Paul Martiny owned three thousand acres. All were in hand and all were farmed excellently. He'd had the capital for modernization and the land paid a decent return on its value. As for the huge and pretentious house he had pulled it down without a pang. The place had been an Edwardian horror and no Preservation Order barred him. He'd built a good modern house and he lived in it comfortably, he and his placid conventional wife. So he didn't need money, he needed escape, relief from a world which would otherwise strangle him. Some men of his kind could find it in sport and others in simple if squalid venery. Paul Martiny was too clever for either; he found his release in acting for criminals in the aspect which mattered most to them, and to criminals this was naturally money. Paul caused money which he knew to be stolen to reappear in other countries; he advised criminals how to invest their loot; he arranged discreet exiles when these became necessary; and occasionally he would handle stones though only when he knew a safe market.

So Martiny ate his lunch and waited. They were eating in one of Rex Lucas's clubs, though club wouldn't have been every man's word for it. It was in fact a high class casino and the food was something more than edible. They were sitting in Lucas's private room, waited on by a very Greek waiter. There'd been smoked eel with a light but pleasant Muscadet, roast duck with an equally solid Morgon. For afterwards there was cheese on the sideboard. That is, if Martiny felt like an afterwards. He was perfectly sure that he would not do so.

He was waiting for Rex Lucas to lead and when it

came over coffee he was quietly surprised. The Greek drank some wine, put his hands on the table. 'It was kind of you to see me,' he said.

'To tell you the truth I was rather intrigued.'

'Let's start at the beginning then. You're related to a man called Horan. Who I gather has done time in jail.'

Martiny was a little uneasy. He hadn't supposed that a man like Lucas would be asking him to accept him as a client. For one thing he wasn't a criminal, or not in the sense of Martiny's contacts, and for another the men he did take on, for ten per cent gross he considered well earned, were secure or they weren't taken on at all. He had turned down more men than he'd ever accepted, but if this Greek knew his secret he'd blackmail him mercilessly.

But he didn't really believe he did for there was a specialized side to Martiny's hobby, the business of slipping money abroad. This last he did through banking cousins, a respectable merchant bank in the City but with a proper contempt for Exchange Control. Rex Lucas might have got wind of that without guessing at other more damaging matters, though why a Greek, pastmasters of fiddling, should approach him for such a service he didn't know.

So probably this wasn't that. Martiny said: 'Horan?' and waited impassively.

'As I said, I believe you're related.'

'No.'

'But you've heard of him?'

'I don't deny it. But we haven't a drop of blood in common.'

The Greek smiled a very Greek smile indeed. 'We

17

Greeks are supposed to be family-conscious, nepotic and I don't know what else. That's perfectly true and I don't apologize. For the English, I've found, are even more so. English, that is, of a certain class.'

'Not conceding I have such a thing, you mean me?'

Rex Lucas used a toothpick discreetly. His teeth were his own still and very white. 'I'm prepared to accept you don't know the relationship. That wouldn't be the English way.'

Paul Martiny let this pass in silence. Like most Englishmen he wasn't happy when foreigners knew too much of the English. 'All I know is that I have a great aunt Lilian. As I hear it she is Horan's too.'

'And is also,' the Greek said, 'extremely wealthy.'

'Again I have heard it.'

'You have no interest?'

Martiny had eaten the Greek's good food but this was a little too much for silence. 'Listen,' he said, and his voice had sharpened. 'I don't think you're as well informed as maybe you've been led to believe— not on the natives' *mores* and ethos. That money was made by a man called Gregg and to a Gregg it will go so long as there is one, not to a distant collateral like me. And Horan's a Gregg on his grandmother's side, the only one left as far as I know. So his great aunt will probably leave him the lot.'

'I'm very glad indeed to hear it. I had heard it as a rumour of course, but I'm delighted to be reassured.'

'May I ask why?'

The Greek looked surprised. 'Of course you may— it's the reason I asked you to do me this honour.' He drank the last of the Morgon, then said almost casually: 'Michael Horan owes me twenty-two thousand.'

'From gambling?' Martiny asked. 'Forget it. We both of us know such a debt's unenforcible.'

'Quite so,' Lucas said, 'I do know that.' His eyes had begun to film and stare but whether from anger or something else Martiny would not have cared to guess. 'It is my turn to return the irony, the one about the natives' customs. Do you gamble, Mr Martiny?'

'Seldom.'

'Then I can understand a certain ignorance. For you cannot run a gambling business and let many debts of that order escape you. The news gets around and defaults increase sharply.'

Paul Martiny nodded, the point was simple. 'So Mike Horan owes you a considerable debt. What I don't understand is how it arose. Twenty-two thousand from a man with no money....'

'I cannot entirely blame my manager. Normally nobody plays at my tables unless guaranteed by another customer, one whose credit is beyond suspicion. But he came in one night with one of these and there has to be some give and take, some discretion which must be exercised wisely. If you try to run high class gambling clubs with the guarantors' paper nailed to the wall you lose clients just as fast and disastrously as you do if you let your defaulters float.'

'Have you tried with the man who introduced him?'

'I have, and he sent me about my business. I don't resent that, he was fully entitled to. He had given no undertaking whatever, nor was he even—mistakenly —asked for one. Moreover he was greatly offended

19

and has taken his custom elsewhere. To my loss.'

'*I'm* not going to pay.'

'I have never suggested it. All I ask is your co-operation.'

'Why should I give it?'

'I'll tell you that.' Rex Lucas's eyes were now almost opaque, but he offered a cigar and lit one. 'In this business there are certain, well, precedents. The first is to send in the frighteners.'

'Pointless in this case.'

'No, not quite. He might have borrowed from that rich friend of his. Who might have felt morally bound to help him.'

'None of these sound very moral people.'

'They have a code of a sort though they don't always live to it. Anyway, Horan couldn't borrow.'

'And then?' Paul asked. But he'd guessed the answer.

For a moment the Greek's eyes almost cleared. 'And now I must confess to misjudgement—not my own and a man has been heavily disciplined. But he ordered in rather more than the frighteners and Horan was handled a little severely. He made it much worse by resisting strongly.'

'A barbarian thing to do,' Paul said. He was Rex Lucas's guest at Rex Lucas's table but at this moment he wasn't concealing contempt.

But the Greek showed no signs of losing his temper, appearing not even to notice the insult. A formidable man, Paul decided.

'So you see why I need your help,' Lucas said. 'I've discovered that you help people widely. Particularly men who've been in prison.'

20

Paul was relieved: this was public knowledge. It gave him an almost perfect cover for his contacts with the criminal world. He had sat on his County Council for years and once he had been a Deputy Lieutenant, but what he was known for was work with ex-prisoners; he sweated on earnest and pompous committees, concealing a patrician distaste for people he mostly considered wet. Those penologists, for instance —stupid. (And what in hell did a penologist *do*?) He'd been horrified when they'd trapped him on telly and the panel had talked for half an hour, not one of them daring to use the word punishment. Paul Martiny wasn't an intellectual, and a criminal who did too much time was a criminal who had failed at his job. There was a price for that as there was for all failure. So it was odious work but it did give him cover, and what he did under cover had hooked him for life. Farming three thousand acres properly, living with placid but boring Matty—he'd go mad without a legitimate safety valve.

He corrected himself—that was hardly the adjective. Never mind that, he'd been born an insider. All the sharper the taste, then, for smashing the idols.

He returned to Rex Lucas, more coolly now. 'I've been rude and I beg your pardon sincerely. So the least I can do is to listen carefully.'

'Good,' Lucas said, 'since it's perfectly simple. It's evident I must wait for my money, but whilst I do so I cannot have Horan too visible, walking about London quite freely. Such things are bad for, well, for discipline. So I'm prepared to pay him forty a week provided he goes abroad and stays there. Forty pounds a week, that is, till his great aunt dies and I get my money. I want you to persuade him to take it.'

'Why not put it to him yourself directly?'

'I dare not. I have done a little research, you see, or rather had the research done for me. Your relation, collateral—call him anything—is a very stubborn man indeed, and also by all accounts a proud one. Moreover, as I confessed before, there was a mistake made and he was beaten up. Could I put a proposition of this sort to the kind of man I believe him to be?'

'I take the point.' Paul Martiny considered. 'One thing occurs to me.'

'I'd be grateful to hear it.'

'You seem very sure that Horan will pay. Strictly it's no business of mine but there's a cliché about throwing good money after bad.'

Rex Lucas smiled patiently. 'Yes, and a wise one. But you'll admit that I wouldn't have met some success if I hadn't known my business thoroughly. You remarked before, and perfectly rightly, that the courts won't recover a debt from gambling. But a gambling debt can change its nature—that's been the law for many years. So A owes B money arising from gambling, but if that debt is discreetly submerged in a contract, an ordinary justiciable contract, that contract can be a perfectly good one. It's tricky as these things mostly are, but I have excellent solicitors—Emersons.'

Paul Martiny let this pass again. Emersons were his own solicitors, one of a dozen great firms in London. Any document they drew would stand up, and that without the expensive advice of barristers who knew less than Emersons. 'You do know your business,' Paul said.

'I need to.'

'And you want me to put this proposal to Horan?'

'I think it would be to our mutual advantage.'

'You realize I've never met him?'

'I do. But you have a standing he hasn't, a certain authority.'

'You oblige me at least to think it over.'

'You will let me know?'

'Within forty-eight hours.'

'That's really very kind indeed.'

Paul Martiny rose. 'I've enjoyed my lunch.'

'And I have enjoyed your company greatly.'

Martiny went back to his room in London. It wasn't so different from Michael Horan's, comfortable but unpretentious, and there he sat down to consider carefully. He had a horror of all casual involvements, both as a matter of solid principle and also from unhappy experience. There'd been that matter of the Reverend Clement, the Reverend Clement Melsome M.A., a first cousin once removed, he remembered, and he'd be happy to see him removed again. He was very High Church in a Low Church diocese, which was Melsome's misfortune, not Paul Martiny's, but there'd been that trouble with a cathedral choirboy, and Paul, who had had a Chief Constable's ear, had felt obliged to use it discreetly. The affair had made him squirm and sweat for it had never been his inclination to stand as the head of a clamorous clan.

But Michael Horan sounded distinctly different from the amours of a High Church clergyman. He'd been to prison, had he? And he'd defended himself with a good deal of courage when it wouldn't have been hard to forgive him if he hadn't chosen to risk resistance. 'Rather more than the frighteners,' Lucas had said, and the plural had not escaped Paul Martiny. That meant two men at least and probably coshes. Horan wouldn't just jump at an offer from Lucas, one which he might rightly decide was a matter of piling insult on injury.

Such a man sounded very well worth a meeting.

Happily Paul could make an inquiry for Michael Horan had been in jail. That meant that one of Martiny's contacts—'clients', he thought, with a secret smile—would be able to find out most of the facts: what Horan had gone to prison for, how long he'd served and how he'd behaved. Above all things whether the others had liked him. Prison, like stuffy and touchy regiments, could be hell on earth if you didn't fit in.

He picked up the phone and made his inquiry. The voice at the other end was brief.

'Give me two days, squire. I'll put it in writing.'

And there was another thing he ought to do, pay a visit again to old Lilian Gregg. He saw her every month or so and not from a sense of pious duty. The old lady had an astringent wit, a cynical humour, and still great elegance. It was rumoured she'd been King Edward's mistress and if she'd gone to him young that was still quite possible. Paul Martiny very greatly admired her and he called on her with a genuine gusto. But he hadn't been for several months. This wasn't because he had changed his mind but because any call had become a gamble. Some days she was still as sharp as a razor but on others she was very near senile. Talking to her then was painful, especially as he really liked her. Like himself, he suspected, she had never conformed. *Grandes dames* seldom felt the need to do so.

He was returning to his house in three days and he'd pay his visit from there, not from London. Westercombe, where Dorothy Tellier kept her exclusive and very expensive Home, was nearer to Paul's house than London and in any case he had brought up no car.

He looked at his watch: it was now six o'clock. He poured himself a generous whisky. He hadn't very much interest in food but he enjoyed a drink though he drank with discipline. He wondered if Charlotte Tellier was in. It was a little late for a casual call and Charlotte could be a stickler for what she considered her menfolk owed her. In many ways rather a dangerous woman and she was certainly very hard indeed, but she kept to the rules, she never pestered. After that week in Venice they'd had she hadn't even rung him up. A fur, he had given her, rather a good one, for the week had been a great success.

He picked up the phone but put it down. He'd decided he didn't really want her.

3

When Martiny had gone Rex Lucas thought hard for he hadn't told all that he knew—far from it. What he'd said had been truthful as far as it went but had concealed what to Lucas was now the essential. He had said he was ready to wait for his money, make arrangements with Horan till Lady Gregg died. *But supposing Mike Horan was not the heir?* In that case Martiny would be perfectly right: Lucas would be wasting good money.

He sighed for his information was scaring; it was reliable too since it came from Emersons. Of course Emersons were much too correct to leak news about other clients' affairs, but their correctness was precisely the point. They acted for many rich men and women, many who used Rex Lucas's tables. It was necessary to know their real standing, whether they were safely rich or survivals with a decaying title. As Lucas had remarked to Martiny you couldn't run high class gambling clubs without knowing your business extremely well.

He paid an articled clerk in the firm of Emersons two thousand a year to keep him informed on the real background of many who played at his tables.

And his latest information was puzzling. Sir Duncan Gregg had also used Emersons and so had his widow till very recently. Then one day there'd been a formal letter, formal and also carefully polite. Lady Gregg was no longer as young as she had been, it was impossible to visit London, so no doubt it would be understood if she felt it more convenient if her legal adviser lived somewhat closer. There were firms which might well have replied to this that they would send a partner down next day but Emersons were too old for that. They had collected the old lady's papers and sent them to Westercombe by hand. They had sent them to Mr Gilbert Heale-Mann.

Lucas hadn't liked the sound of it. He could think of only a single reason for Lilian Gregg to change her lawyers and that was to make another Will. When Emersons might have shied like stallions, asking all manner of awkward questions as any good lawyer was bound to do.... Had she really considered this in full, the implications and the final results?

And privately, though they wouldn't say so, was she fit to make a new Will at all? Rex Lucas had frowned for he knew some law, as he knew something of half a dozen professions. Testamentary capacity, then: it was something which was always tricky with any person who lived under permanent care.

So any good solicitor would ask many and often searching questions but a rogue might have other plans and skip them. Rex Lucas had checked on Heale-Mann with care but he didn't appear any sort of shyster; he appeared, on the contrary, somewhat stuffy. His firm had been in Westercombe for something like a hundred years, founded by a grandfather who at that time had been simply Mann. But the son had married a local heiress and now it was Heale-Mann—much grander. The present Mr Gilbert Heale-Mann had hunted until he grew too stiff, and he gave charming little dinner parties which were sought after by more than his clients. Such a man didn't sound an adventurer, and almost certainly he'd be much too clever to be looking for any money directly. But there were other and much more devious motives.

Rex Lucas sighed for the second time. He needed not speculation on motive but hard knowledge of how the position stood. He pressed his intercom and barked at it sharply.

'Send me up George,' he said.

'Which George?'

'The fat one.' Lucas used more than one man called George. He would in fact use anyone provided he had an adequate hold on him and on Fat George he had the best of all, a knowledge of several crimes undetected.

When George arrived Lucas looked at him critically but he waved him to a chair in the end. He was certainly getting exceedingly stout, good living was taking an evident toll, but he still had his skills and these were valuable. 'It's information I want.'

'What sort of gen?'

'It's legal information.'

'Wrong number. I was a lawyer once but I never practised.'

'I know perfectly well why you never practised. But I'll confess that I was putting it badly. In point of fact it's not legal advice but information about a couple of Wills to be found in a certain solicitor's office.'

'You need a peterman to blow a safe.'

'You're really being a little tiresome. You've been in England a long time now but you don't seem to know very much of the people. This is a country solicitor—very—and though country solicitors do have safes they only use them for the stuff that matters, money for instance or bearer bonds, the occasional paper they feel is important. The rest is kept in filing drawers or even in absurd tin boxes if the man is the really old-fashioned kind. Boxes with locks a child could pick and legends on the top in white paint like *In re The Gallops, The Buttermould Settlement*.'

'I still think it's a job for a specialist.'

'What would I gain by sending a peterman? He wouldn't understand these Wills, so he'd either have to steal them both, which would certainly be noticed quite soon, or else he'd have to take a camera, and flashbulbs at night might be noticed too. But you can understand the jargon, and as I told you these drawers or boxes are child's play.'

'I think you said Wills.'

'I did and I meant it. I need to know who benefits on the death of a lady called Lilian Gregg. I think I know what the first Will provides but I'm very uneasy about the second.'

'Let me think,' George said. He had spoken in Greek. Up to now they had been speaking in English, not because their Greek was rusty but because George's Cypriot accent offended. Fat George lit a cigarette and waited. He was playing hard to get —more money. He said at length:

'What sort of solicitor?'

'A country solicitor—I've already told you. The name is Heale-Mann and they're down at Westercombe. It's a watering place on the North Devon coast. They operate in the central square, an old

Georgian house called Stable House. Do what I ask and it's worth two hundred.'

'Paid in advance,' Fat George said promptly. He didn't trust Rex Lucas an inch and indeed there were not very many who did.

'Half in advance.'

'No, all or nothing.'

Rex Lucas didn't like this at all but finally passed across the money. Fat George put it in his wallet neatly, then went back to the business still in hand.

'You're quite sure that these Wills won't be in a safe?'

'If they are I shall have to think again but I don't suppose I shall really have to. So you look in any filing cabinet which covers the letter G. Lady Gregg. Or they might be in one of those foolish boxes. If it helps you she's the widow of a scoundrel called Sir Duncan Gregg, Baronet.'

'Checking on what you want to know—'

'I want to know who inherits her money. If there's only one Will that's a man called Horan but if there are two it might be anyone.' Lucas looked at Fat George with a sudden query. 'You can manage the locks without breaking them open?'

'Oh yes, I can manage office locks. If I couldn't I might be a practising lawyer.'

'Then do it tonight.'

'I can't do that. I've a date to take a lady to dinner.' Fat George allowed a self-satisfied leer. 'Very superior bird indeed. I doubt if I'll make her tonight but I will. French-sounding name—something like Tellier. Not that she's as grand as she says. Her mother keeps a Home for the Elderly.'

30

'If she's a grain of sense she'll eat your dinner, then she'll thank you on her doorstep politely. I doubt if you'll ever see her again though in any case you won't tonight. Tonight I said and I mean tonight.'

'No bird's worth two hundred. I'll do it tonight.'

Rex Lucas had thought that Fat George still had skills, and George drove sedately west to use them. He had never practised his chosen profession for he'd been caught with his hand in the till almost literally. He'd always been greatly interested in the way people kept their papers and valuables and the average lock held no secrets whatever. This had started as little more than a hobby but the hobby had become worth money and Fat George had gone close to professional standards. Not quite up to them since he'd never wished to. A real peterman's was a dangerous trade: the courts could give you swingeing sentences and if you made a mistake you could easily maim yourself. Besides, he had delicate nerves, hated noises. But the only doubt he'd ever had about this evening's work which would earn him two hunderd was that Rex Lucas might have been optimistic. He was prepared to believe that country solicitors were old-fashioned and, by his own standards, careless, but it sounded as though they were also untidy. It was all very well to direct him airily to a filing drawer which was marked with a G or a box painted handsomely *Lady Gregg*. Either would be easy enough but only assuming he found one or the other, and in a messy and probably casual office that might not be as easy to do as Rex Lucas had blandly assumed it would be. The problem as Fat George had assessed it was not opening a simple lock but finding the proper lock to open.

And he hadn't unlimited time to do it. It wouldn't be safe to start before midnight and country towns came to life pretty early.

He had driven down to Westercombe not too greatly regretting Charlotte Tellier. There was more than one Charlotte knocking round London and another would certainly come his way. He arrived at half past eleven at night. It wasn't the season, the town was dead. He drove to the central square and parked, leaving his leading wheels pointing outwards. That could save you two seconds which were sometimes important.

He cased the old Georgian house with care. Once it had been a burgher's home or perhaps the town house of some local notable, but now it was offices —Stable House. He saw at once that breaking in was no problem whatever—the place invited it. The only thing which troubled him was a light on the second floor, the solicitor's. It would hardly be any kind of nightwatchman, this wasn't the sort of town which employed them, and he decided that someone had left a switch on. Just the same he'd have to investigate before he started on any serious work.

He opened a back window contemptuously, killing the old-fashioned alarm. He was in some sort of doctor's waiting-room, identifiable by dusty copies of *Woman* and of *Country Life*. He walked through the unlocked door to the hall, then carefully felt his way up the stairs. At their head was a landing and Fat George halted. On his left was a pair of green baize doors which he felt certain would lead to the general offices; on his right was a more important door and underneath it a thin ribbon of light.

32

Fat George went up to it, totally silent. He was a very stout man but could move like a cat. For an instant he used his torch, then dowsed it, for the second of light had been enough. On the door was a fine brass plate, well polished. It said simply:

MR GILBERT HEALE-MANN.

Fat George stood stiller than ever, listening. At first he heard nothing and then it came, the sound of a regular gentle snoring.

Fat George allowed his first smile of the evening. That light was now explained reassuringly. Mr Gilbert Heale-Mann had been working late, Mr Gilbert Heale-Mann had dropped off at his desk.

He slipped across the landing again to the swing doors which led to the general office. The lock was no better than George had expected and he opened it in under four minutes. He went inside and used his torch cautiously. There were a dozen or so filing cabinets and he soon found the drawers which covered G.

But he didn't find anything covering Gregg.

He was disappointed but by no means hopeless. The filing system had not been meticulous and there was still another room to search. At the far side of the general office was another door and this one was unlocked. It was the sanctum of some managing clerk and the desk was a very fine piece of furniture. The walls on three sides were piled with tin boxes, neatly lettered as Lucas had said they would be—*The Honourable Mrs Droxford*, *The Weston Estate* and many others. They were piled one on top of the other awkwardly and he couldn't risk any sort of noise. It took him an hour to confirm what he'd feared: there was nothing here either on Lady Gregg.

He went back to the landing and stood considering, not what he must do since he knew that already but how he could do it best, with least noise. He never carried a gun or cosh and in any case was much to stout to start mixing it even with elderly gentlemen. But he had a valuable weapon and that was surprise. Wake an ageing man from a sleep at his desk and it was unlikely that he'd react with violence. On the contrary he'd be shocked and timid.

Fat George listened at the door again. The snoring still rose and fell like a tide. He sleeps pretty hard, Fat George thought—lucky. I've lost more than an hour and a half already.

So far, though he'd been wearing gloves, he hadn't bothered to put on a mask. Now he put on a hood which he knew looked alarming. So much the better since alarm was his ally.

He eased the door open and went in quietly. Heale-Mann had his head down across his desk and if Fat George hadn't heard his peaceful snoring he might have suspected worse than sleep. He said sharply:

'Good morning. Sit up but don't move.' He had the fat man's characteristic squeak but he was pitching his voice as low as he could.

For a second Heale-Mann did nothing whatever, then he acted with what for a man of his age was immediate and astonishing speed. He didn't waste time in futile speech but sat up as he had been told to do. A second ago he'd been fast asleep but now he was very awake indeed. He dropped his right hand and felt for a drawer; he pulled it half open and there it stuck.

Fat George could also think fast when he had to. He threw his seventeen stone across the desk and his head caught Heale-Mann on the point of the chin. Heale-Mann had reached the gun by now but it fell to the floor as he slid there himself.

Fat George rolled off the desk; he was wheezing. He had a vast distaste for this sort of action, and the last thing but one he had ever wanted was a struggle for a gun which he'd lose. The ultimate last was a slug in his belly. To shoot a man who had not yet threatened you was something which no court would approve, but this man was a solicitor and he'd be believed when he told his brazen lies. Fat George had been lucky a second time but now he'd have to work very fast. Heale-Mann was out but how long he would stay so was something Fat George didn't wish to bet on.

He took Heale-Mann's keys from his silver chain and opened the drawers of his desk one by one. The third on the left held the file he was looking for. There were indeed two Wills and he skimmed them. The first, much the older and drawn by Emersons, left most of the spoils to a man called Horan, the second, barely a fortnight written (so that was why it was still in a desk) left everything to a Clement Melsome. It had been drawn by the man who was now on the floor and had been witnessed by himself and a doctor.

Short, Fat George thought, and distinctly sweet. Sweet, that is, for this Clement Melsome. In any case he now had what he'd come for. Rex Lucas would be very pleased but that wouldn't mean there'd be extra money. Fat George knew that from long experience.

He put the papers back in the drawer and locked it, returning the keys to Heale-Mann's pocket. Then he robbed Heale-Mann of watch and wallet, a silver cigarette case and lighter. He'd been lucky again, very lucky indeed. Heale-Mann wouldn't even guess what he'd come for, he'd simply assume he'd been vulgarly robbed. Fat George picked up the two-two also. It was a weapon for a woman's handbag but any firearm in London was always worth money. No doubt Heale-Mann would report its loss since this gun was almost certainly licensed, but the man who would buy it would probably not be ... Some old pensioner alone in a crumbling house, surrounded by a decaying suburb—would *he* get a licence? By God he would not! But a solicitor in respectable practice, knowing the Bench and the senior policemen.... He didn't need a gun but he had one.

So Fat George picked it up and took it too. He had friends more deserving than Gilbert Heale-Mann. He had two hundred pounds for a simple night's work but he wasn't a man to decline a bonus.

Charlotte Tellier was talking to Clement Melsome. He was her fiancé and she didn't like him but she had perfectly read Clement Melsome's character. With men like this there was only one way. You told them some of the truth and then put your foot down. 'It's all right,' she was saying, 'my mother's arranged it.'

'You mean about the old lady's money?'

'What else could I mean?'

'It troubles my conscience.'

She looked up at him, but hiding her anger. What a wet he was, a High Anglican wet! She'd heard rumours about a choirboy too, but if true then she reckoned she'd break him of that. She was desirable and very experienced. Not that she'd have to suffer him long, just a couple of years and then the dressing-room. A man of his kind would hardly kick, or if he did he would kick in the feeblest way. He couldn't divorce her, a High Church creep, so there'd be some sort of Deed of Separation and of course a very generous covenant. With that money he could afford one easily. Then she'd buy herself something somewhere with sun and in that sun she would live as she'd always wished to.

She remembered that it had been very hard work to bring Reverend Clement up to it. Even now it wasn't quite clear what had happened. Had he proposed to her or vice versa? It was a difficult point, perhaps semantic, but the fact remained he had bought her a ring. She was formally his fiancée now, and God how she had needed him.

For she was a realist and could face the facts. Her bread came from a modest job, a little butter from what her mother gave her from the lush pickings she made in her Home for the Elderly. But to live as she wished she had needed men and the sort of man she'd consider marrying had never come up to the line and asked her. She was much too worldly to think this strange. The man she wanted, very simply a rich one, would scarcely assume she was *virgo intacta*. Rich men were on the whole the more tolerant, they would expect and accept a certain, well, usage, but there was a difference between that and plain shop-soiling. She had realized she had come near to the limit when two men at a party had looked at her strangely. Neither had said an offensive word, if anything they'd been slightly too courteous, but Charlotte had read the signals clearly. She was dangerously near an appalling edge and once you went over you never got back.

And anyway she was thirty-two, she couldn't go on much longer like this ... That fat Cypriot Greek who had asked her to dinner. She would never have let him near her bed but she'd been reluctant to turn down an excellent meal, the prospect of a new fish on the hook. In the end he had stood her up, not she him.

She had met Clement Melsome at Cala Viñas. He had been with another clergyman, both of them on package tours, and she had been with a gentleman friend. But he'd been rather an important gentleman and had been staying in a different hotel. Charlotte had been glad of this for her experienced eye had spotted Clement. His friend had been wearing a wedding ring but neither of them wore clerical collars. She had thought him well-to-do but not rich: both had been talking of houses too big for them. Later she had heard the word 'Rectory' and at first it had put her off completely. But why not an old-fashioned, ample Rectory? Many were minor country houses. In any case she couldn't be choosey. Once, perhaps, she could have. Not now.

Then she had heard a second phrase and that phrase had been 'Old Lilian Gregg'. Charlotte Tellier had moved in at once. The hotel had been free and easy, classless, a sort of holiday camp in Majorcan sun, and to talk to a man without introduction wasn't thought of as a social crime. In the event she'd contrived a clumsy dive and though she'd hurt Clement Melsome it was he who apologized. Plain sailing after that, too easy, and it hadn't been more than a couple of days before they were taking their lunch at a single table. Dinner she had elsewhere with her gentleman.

So casually she had thrown the name back. Had she heard Clement mention a Lilian Gregg?

Very possibly. He certainly knew one.

The one who lived at Westercombe?

Yes.

An extraordinary coincidence, really. That's why she'd brought it up at all. Lilian lived in the Home her mother kept.

Clement Melsome had bowed too stiffly but smiled. 'Then I'm really very grateful to you. I know that she's very well cared for indeed.'

'That's really very sweet of you.' She gave him an enchanting smile; she could still pull great charm when she chose to do so. 'Are you related, then?'

'No, not really. I'm some sort of distant connection by marriage. The old lady had a younger sister who married into the Martiny family and the Melsomes tie up with Martinys somewhere.'

'The Melsomes,' she thought—he had said it so smugly, almost as though he wasn't a clergyman but a proper man with a job amongst men.

'Then you *are* related.'

'It depends how you define the word.'

She found him almost intolerably pompous but she was prepared to pay a very high price.

So Mother had badgered old Lady Gregg into signing a Will in Clement's favour. Put baldly like that it sounded extraordinary, a man whose name she had hardly recognized, but Lilian Gregg had her very bad days and Mrs Tellier had been cruelly insistent. As for the legal side that had been easy for she'd been living with Gilbert Heale-Mann for years. Nobody had even guessed and in a small town like Westercombe that was a triumph. But then she was a clever woman, and Charlotte's streak of ruthlessness descended from a ruthless mother.

So Dorothy Tellier had not been scrupulous; she'd held a pistol at Heale-Mann's respectable head. Do as I wish or face a scandal. I can face one and ride it out all right; I only keep a Home for the Elderly. But you're a solicitor in a country practice and you've very much more to lose than I have. When you retire you'll go on the Bench, or rather I know that that's what you want. That and three letters after your name.

Heale-Mann had kicked but in the end had submitted. He had done what Dorothy Tellier asked him. He had known there were risks but he'd tried to cover them. He couldn't make any new Will quite watertight, not for a woman of ninety-plus who lived in a Home under medical care, but the witnesses to the new Will he'd drawn had been himself and the doctor who saw her weekly.

The doctor had owed him a good deal of money. Westercombe was entirely typical of the apparently simple and bluff West Country.

And now, Charlotte thought, this stupid man. This bloody man could ruin everything. Talking about his conscience indeed! He wasn't entitled to have such a thing.

40

4

Paul Martiny's contact had kept his word and Paul now had Horan's history on paper. But before he read it again with greater care there was something else which he ought to check; he ought to check where he stood on the tree with Horan. To do so he went to his wife Matilda. Matty's father had married a German in Germany and she had all of that race's uneasy passion for genealogy and family trees.

Her own and her husband's too by now.

She told him at once without looking at papers. His grandmother—his maternal grandmother—had had a sister called Lilian who had married a Gregg. He hadn't been a baronet then but a Dundonian on the make in jute. Matilda hadn't said so in terms but she'd contrived to convey what Paul guessed was a fact, that his own family had had private doubts. But later this Gregg had made a great fortune so everything had blown over agreeably. Matilda Martiny had sounded tolerant. England wasn't like her mother's country where status was much more fixed and immutable.

... This Gregg then—what had happened afterwards?

Well, he'd piled up a fortune in jute in Calcutta but he'd never begotten children by Lilian. By all accounts she hadn't been faithful; she'd had many affairs in improbable places, though Matty herself didn't credit the rumour that she'd once been a King of England's mistress. But she had been around, yes she certainly had, but somehow she had never tarnished. She'd always been clever, she'd kept an air, and later as she grew older and richer the aura of a great lady had shielded her. It was a pity that she had never had children but she did have an heir on her husband's side.

Because Duncan Gregg had had a sister who had married into the Glasgow Irish. The Greggs had disliked the marriage intensely, for they were Lowlanders and bitterly Protestant. But this girl had run away and married and the name of the man she had married was Horan. They had had a son and he another. Their own son was dead but the grandson wasn't. His name was apparently Michael Horan, and Matty, who'd had little interest in him, knew nothing about him except he existed.

Paul had thanked her politely and gone to his study, where he read his contact's report more carefully.... An unusual story, a very unusual one. He wondered what a psychiatrist would make of the tale which this contact had sent him. Probably something excessively learned and certainly extremely misleading. To Paul one aspect stood out quite clearly; he and this distant connection Horan had more in common than simply a great aunt. Neither would stand for being leant on.

He'd think about that later, though. For the moment he must consider the facts.

And they followed a pattern which Paul thought logical. Mike Horan had not been expensively educated and had signed as a private for three years' service. Paul Martiny had approved his choice for he'd chosen a famous but civilized regiment, not the sort where the Majors were called 'Sir' in the Mess and where soldiers were taught to stamp and shout.

So a civilized regiment and just as well, since something had gone very wrong indeed. Paul's informant was not very certain what. There was a rumour about a bullying sergeant but the writer couldn't pretend to confirm it. All that was known was a couple of facts, that Horan had been severely punished and of course he hadn't received his commission.

So he'd done his three years in the ranks and come out again at a time when it hadn't been hard to find decent work provided you didn't set sights too high. He had gone as a clerk to Wallis and Williamson, another of the great London solicitors, every bit as prestigious as Emersons were and in their own way every bit as stuffy. A partner had liked the look of Mike Horan, his pleasant manners but more than these his air of a man who was still uncorrupted. Such men were always difficult and often they were actively dangerous, but one couldn't withhold a real respect. So after a year there'd been talk of Articles but it hadn't worked out like that in the end.

For Wallis and Williamson, very blue-blooded, had clients who sometimes had vulgar problems. What did you do when a major tycoon came in and complained of industrial espionage? He was an important client, a very rich man, so you couldn't just tell him this wasn't your line. He would expect, and was entitled to, that at least you would give him a contact. You did so. There was a firm of detectives which specialized in counter-industrial spying and leakages and Wallis and Williamson had used them before.

With success but of course there were always snags. This firm was manned by tough ex-policemen and a man like Sir John might not feel quite happy to lay all his cards down (he'd have to do that) in a game where the rules were sometimes uncertain. Nor for that matter were Wallis and Williamson, though they'd found this firm extremely useful in other matters than counter-espionage. But suppose they could slip in a man they could trust, a man who had learnt a little law and who in any case owed them a generous start. A man of their own—in short Michael Horan. Then they could use these ex-policemen with confidence; they could even advise Sir John to go to them.

Mike Horan had thought hard but accepted; he had joined the ex-policemen and soon found his feet. Wallis and Williamson guaranteed he should do so since they sent this concern a good deal of work and now were prepared to send more and more delicate, the sort which earned the really big money. But not for Mike Horan, it hadn't gone right for him....

Michael Horan had been seeing his man by appointment, one made for him by Sir John himself. Otherwise he would not have obtained it.

He looked round the handsome office curiously. It said family business a trifle aggressively. This was where a man worked since he had to work but his real interests were in his sports and hobbies. There were pictures on the wall of yachts and it was late on a Friday afternoon. The director wore a reefer jacket with brass buttons with an impressive crest. He was ready to leave for a weekend's sailing and when

Michael came in he had looked at his watch. He didn't say: 'I can give you five minutes' but the look at his watch had said the same. Michael Horan resented the air of patronage.

'What can I do for you?'

'I'd just like you to listen.'

Horan told him what he had painfully learnt over two or three months of very hard slogging. This company had been taken over by the conglomerate which Sir John now headed but not all the Board had won golden handshakes. Two men had remained and were known to be bitter, men connected with what before the takeover had been a family firm for generations. And one of them was leaking badly, leaking to a rival company. Mike Horan had found out which director. His evidence wouldn't stand up in a court but then it didn't have to stand up. Sir John hadn't wanted that—no indeed. There'd been too many City scandals already. So his instructions had been clear and succinct. He wanted this man to resign, off the Board, and thereafter there'd be no prosecution. Bluff was what was needed—firmness and bluff. Sir John had been complimentary; he believed Mike Horan had both these talents and if he pulled off this mission, admittedly difficult, Sir John would show a material gratitude.

Michael Horan inspected his man as he talked. He didn't look the sort to break easily. Under his tiresome reefer jacket he was thickset and powerful; he weighed fully fifty pounds more than Michael. His face was red with the broken veins of a man who was thirty years his senior. It was evident that his private interests were not confined to sailing boats.

When Michael had finished the director was silent. Then he said dangerously: 'Prove that in court.'

'We needn't even try to prove it. Sir John doesn't want to.'

'Sir John?'

'That is so. You must have guessed whom I'm acting for since it was he who made the appointment to call.'

'Then what does he want?'

'Your resignation.'

'And if I refuse it?'

'He'll vote you out. His company owns this one a hundred per cent. If that happens you'll never work again.'

The thickset man in the reefer jacket showed his teeth in an unbecoming snarl. He looked at Mike Horan's card on his desk. 'Horan,' he said. 'You're a bloody Mick.'

'In point of fact I was born in Glasgow.'

'Where they're born doesn't matter much to bastards.'

'Then the answer to Sir John is No?'

'I don't care a curse what you tell Sir John. But I'll teach you a lesson before you go.'

So far Mike Horan had kept his temper and he might have still held it hard on rein if the thickset man hadn't risen furiously. He came behind Michael's chair and lifted him. He did it with ease and a clear contempt for he was a very powerful man indeed. He lifted Mike below the armpits, then he threw him against the office door.

Horan picked himself up; he still had his temper. Only just but he was still in control. He felt for the knob of the door behind him. He didn't want trouble, he wanted out.

He felt for the knob but he didn't find it for the thickset man had knocked him down. It wasn't a scientific punch but it had fifteen stone of flesh behind it and it had been well below the official belt. Michael lay still till he got his breath back, dodging the very inexpert kicks. Then he climbed to his feet, took the big man to pieces. He did it with venom, a genuine gusto. It didn't occur till afterwards that he'd done very much more than the law would think proper.

... Paul Martiny, reading the ghost of this, felt the sharp goad of a lively sympathy. Horan had over-reacted insanely but the sentence in that court had been savage.

Martiny didn't admire the courts. A court of law made him physically ill, even the local magistrates' bench which he'd steadfastly refused to sit on. It racked his nerves, it stirred his bile. He wasn't consciously an iconoclast, and if the national game was controlled by backwoodsmen, if senior churchmen were clearly senile, he didn't burn up to pull them down. But it reinforced his natural instinct that this establishment he'd been born into was very near its final end. Open protest in absurd processions was pointless and it was also undignified. It did nothing but astonish the bourgeois, which was something which only satisfied children, whereas if by birth you were inside the wall you could sap at it without foolish posing. It was even, in its compulsive thrust, a pleasure to do just that. Paul took it. He took it by managing criminals' earnings, covering his dangerous contacts by posing as a Bleeding Heart, a man wholly committed to ex-Prisoners' Aid.

Paul Martiny smiled—Horan wasn't his client. For one thing he wasn't a proper criminal, simply a man with a wicked temper; he certainly wasn't a well-off professional whose profits would stand ten per cent and make it worth Paul's while to accept him. And Paul hated the smell of all involvement, emotional involvement especially. He would have given the twenty thousand he'd earned from a famous but still unpunished haul to feel free to let this Horan be. That he couldn't was nothing to do with crime and certainly not with a great aunt in common. He realized that what he felt was personal, a feeling for his own kind of man. This Horan had very strong blood—that was evident. Paul Martiny knew what that meant: it meant trouble.... We're both fishes in the establishment net and the mesh is too fine to wriggle through. Then you bit through it yourself and escaped. Could you leave another with less strong teeth to be landed by the establishment fishermen? You could, no doubt, but you'd always despise yourself.

Martiny's contact had done his work thoroughly and at the bottom of the two sheets of foolscap was Michael Horan's address in London. Something about it was faintly familiar: wasn't that the address of Charlotte Tellier? Paul checked it in his address book. Yes. It wasn't what fools would call a smart one, but it was respectable, even modestly cosy. Horan must have saved some money before that blood of his had again betrayed him.

Paul started to write but changed his mind. He could put it in a letter clearly but he could also earn the sort of brush-off which it would be difficult to reverse or heal. Instead he inquired for Mike Horan's number and when he had it he rang through at once.

A polite voice answered. 'Michael Horan here.'

'My name's Paul Martiny. Does that ring a bell?'

'It does ring a faint one. You're some sort of relation.'

'I'd be grateful if you could spare me ten minutes.'

'To tell me I'm a disgrace to the family?' The voice was now ironical but it wasn't in the least offended.

To this pleasantry Paul had a crushing answer but not one he could blurt out to a stranger. 'I don't feel like that about people's misfortunes.'

There was a silence: Horan was clearly thinking. 'Very well,' he said, 'and when would suit you?'

'Tomorrow?'

'At six o'clock. I'll be here to meet you.'

5

Since he'd grown too stiff to enjoy his hunting Mr
Gilbert Heale-Mann had kept fit by walking. He did
so as a matter of discipline and he usually walked the
same course every evening. He climbed the path to
the top of the cliff and then down again. At the
bottom, where the cliff path started, was a pleasant
pub where he took a drink. Often his friend the doctor
joined him, for he also walked in the evening to air
his dog.

Heale-Mann walked briskly, conscious of duty, but
he also used this time to think. He was reconciled
now, or almost reconciled, to the fact that he'd been
unscrupulously blackmailed into drafting a Will
which he hadn't wished to. If Dorothy blew their
little secret it would certainly do him no good in
Westercombe. It mightn't destroy his practice totally
but it would surely destroy his private ambitions.
Dorothy had been right about these. He wanted to
go on the Bench, to be recognized, to be something
more than a country solicitor, and he wouldn't do
that if his formal retirement coincided with a local
scandal. He'd lived here all his life in Westercombe,
he knew the smell of it and the local ethos. As for
the doctor he'd taken to sign with him, he hadn't
exactly blackmailed him in turn, but the doctor had
been more than anxious to fall in with the plans of
a man he owed money to. It wasn't an enormous
amount, Heale-Mann was too canny to lend such a

sum, but it would be a very awkward one to repay. Heale-Mann had never put this in terms for both men had lived long in Westercombe. Both accepted its air of placid propriety, both knew perfectly what the cool mask hid—envy, inherited malice and hatred.

At the pub at the bottom Heale-Mann slipped in. He himself didn't drink until after his walk but the doctor would often go in for a stiffener.

'Doctor ahead of me?'

'Four or five minutes, sir.' The landlord had been obsequious for both of these men were regular customers.

Heale-Mann began his climb reflectively. By now he'd not only accepted the blackmail but had almost managed to justify an action which at first had shamed him.... Who was this Horan they'd cut out of inheritance? A man who'd been to prison, a criminal. It was wrong that great wealth should go to him merely because a rich old woman was too frail to understand the facts if you tried to explain the position normally. Normal—that was a comforting word. When the circumstances were far from normal a certain degree of abnormality was justified if it prevented a wrong. As for this Melsome who'd now get the money, Heale-Mann had never needed to meet him, but from what he had heard he had reservations. Heale-Mann was evangelical and disapproved strongly of High Church caperings, but at least the man was a beneficed priest, a part of the establishment, settled. He'd heard rumours but discounted them. Every unmarried High Anglican priest was suspect of the very same thing and as often as not the suspicions were groundless. In any case Melsome was getting married.

Yes, on every score a better candidate than a man who was a violent criminal.

Heale-Mann had almost persuaded himself that he'd done the only possible thing.

So he began his climb, his mind almost at peace. At first the path was gravelled and lighted, as far as a sort of belvedere with a platform and a wooden hut, but beyond it was the natural rock tramped out by the feet of generations to the summit where the view was much finer. This part of the track was still unlighted and you were foolhardy enough to risk it at night unless you knew the footholds well, but Heale-Mann had been here a hundred times and tonight there was a near full moon. The view from the top across the bay would be sensational in its solemn magnificence.

He climbed on steadily, puffing slightly, remembering that the local Council had been fussing about that rail at the top. Below it was a five hundred foot drop, and though it had once been perfectly adequate the wood was now old and believed to be suspect. Not that anyone but a perfect fool would sit on it or even lean.

The clearing was now ten feet above him but the path was winding round a shoulder. He couldn't yet see it.

Not see but hear. There was a sudden and despairing scream, an outrage on the majestic night. Heale-Mann began to run. He slipped. He picked himself up and ran again. In the clearing the rail had fallen drunkenly, shattered to pieces between two uprights. The doctor's hunt terrier sat on her haunches, howling at the immaculate moon.

52

Heale-Mann was not ashamed he was terrified. He called the doctor's name three times, knowing that each time was pointless. He tried to pick up the shivering bitch. She bit him. He thought he sensed a movement behind him but turning saw nothing move but the gorse.

He shivered himself and went back to the pub. There he used the telephone and soon men were moving along the shore.

6

Paul hadn't been planning a trip to London but he was a man who grasped his nettles firmly. He made his excuses to Matty, his wife, who received them with the polite indifference of a woman whose husband slept in the dressing-room but would never conceivably break up his family, and he motored up to London next day. He left his car in the Kensington square illegally, chancing a fine he could well afford, aware that the action was anti-social but caring nothing whatever for that. Since he broke big laws boldly and showed a profit he wouldn't bother with mere regulations.

He used the speaker at the apartment's front door and Mike Horan answered and freed the lock. Paul Martiny climbed to the first-floor landing, smiling a smile of recognition. This was indeed where Charlotte Tellier lived and for a moment he considered a call when he'd finished his business with Michael Horan. But he decided that he'd do no such thing. She'd been marvellous value, no trouble afterwards, but her charm for an experienced male had been the charm of a brilliant but clearly flawed diamond. It had fascinated Paul Martiny for she didn't seem aware it existed, but this charm had been one which could fade rather quickly. So he didn't want to pick the threads up, it would be foolish to knock on that door, maybe worse.

Instead he knocked on Michael Horan's and a piano

inside stopped the E flat Nocturne. Paul Martiny knew very little of music but his impression had been that Mike Horan played well. The door opened and Horan asked:

'Paul Martiny?'

He nodded assent.

'Please to come in, cousin.'

'I don't think I'm really that, you know.'

'You can hardly say: "Come in, collateral."'

Martiny began to like this man. He put him at thirty-four or five and he spoke with a hint of un-southern precision. To Martiny, who loathed news-readers' English, this was a point in his favour at once.

'A drink?' Horan said.

'That's very kind. Whisky and soda, perhaps. No ice.'

'I'll join you,' Horan said and did so.

He waited silently for Paul to lead but Paul looked round the comfortable room. The furniture was old and charming, the piano looked a very good one. Mike Horan read his thought and smiled.

'If you're thinking I'm flush for a man out of prison you're partly right—I've saved some money. Enough to last six months perhaps, and when it's gone I'll find a job. I doubt if it will be a good one but meantime I'm living a life I enjoy.'

Paul nodded again; he thought this sensible. There wasn't any sort of virtue in working if you didn't have to. Plenty of people believed the opposite but they weren't Paul Martiny's sort of people. Matilda Martiny would probably be one but Matty's mother had been a German.

'Another whisky?' Horan suggested.

'Not for the moment—let's wait and see. To tell you the truth I've an awkward hunch that I'm drinking your drink under false pretences.'

'We could settle that by your telling me everything. Why you've looked me up and your private motive.'

Martiny's liking for Mike was increasing. 'Have you heard of a man called Rex Lucas?'

'Certainly.' Mike Horan wasn't hiding surprise. 'I shouldn't have thought you would even know him.'

'I've only met him once in my life but we do have an acquaintance in common. This acquaintance fixed a meeting at luncheon. A pretty good luncheon it was at that. At it Lucas told me a story.'

'About myself?'

'About yourself.'

'I'm afraid it was probably perfectly true. I went to one of his places one night and there I lost money I didn't have. It was a stupid thing to do. I regret it. I didn't need money—I told you I'd saved some— and I'm not a man with an itch to gamble. What I am alas is a Celt. I lose my head.'

'Your visitors left you that,' Paul said.

'So he told you that too—the frighteners and later the strongarms? They beat me up quite severely, you know, but I dare say it was largely my fault. I fought back.'

'Who wouldn't?'

'A sensible man would not have fought back. Unhappily I'm not a sensible man.'

'One of the messages Lucas gave me was that the beating was done without his knowledge. I was to tell you he was sorry it happened.'

'Tell Lucas what to do with that.' It mightn't be telly but it was fully explicit.

Paul Martiny laughed. 'My own feeling exactly. But that wasn't the only message he gave me.'

'No?' Horan said. His voice held a warning but Paul went on.

'And I confess the man seemed to have a point. To me, that is, and perhaps to you.' Paul Martiny leant forward to make his own. 'Try to put yourself in Rex Lucas's place. . . . A man walks into one of his houses and loses twenty-two thousand he doesn't have. So the frighteners come and later the strong-arms. The former, I gather, are normal routine, and as for the latter you make your own choice whether Lucas knew or Lucas didn't. But one thing which he can't afford is to have bilkers walking freely round London. Let that happen and his business suffers. Twenty-two thousand is hardly chickenfeed.'

'And so?' Horan asked.

'So his second message. He will pay you forty pounds a week provided you go abroad for a bit.'

'Which implies he believes he will get his money.'

'He seemed confident he would get his money. This allowance he offers—we'll call it that—would be tied up in some form of legal contract and he knows that you have expectations.'

'Does he indeed. May I ask you how?'

'I confirmed it myself.'

'That was pretty cool.' It was a statement of fact, not one made in anger.

'I think it will protect your skin. If he thinks that he'll get paid in time his interest is to play you gently, not send bullyboys to knock you about.'

'You seem pretty sure I shall get this money.'

'For the same reason I gave that loathsome Greek. My grandmother's sister had perhaps a small dowry but it wouldn't have been that sort of money. What her husband piled up was Gregg money—Gregg. You have Gregg blood and I have none. Moreover I happen to own what I need and it wouldn't attract me to stack up more merely to have it stolen in Duty.'

'You're not a socialist, then?'

'I am certainly not. But the other lot makes me even sicker.'

Mike Horan rose, pouring second whiskies. 'No question of false pretences. Join me.' He brought Paul Martiny his drink and sat down again. 'So that was the message—forty a week. Now the advice, please.'

'I'm not going to give any. I didn't undertake to press you, only to put the proposition.'

'I can see that Rex Lucas couldn't put it directly.' Horan touched his head lightly, half in apology. 'I've an excellent doctor who keeps his mouth shut but my neck still aches in the evening badly and in the morning I'm still as stiff as a post.'

'There's a risk if you refuse, you know.'

'On what you've now told me it's not a big one. I don't believe what Lucas told you, that the beating was done without his knowledge, but I do believe he's now thinking sensibly. Hurting me won't produce a penny; on the contrary I might turn nasty. I might wait till aunt Lilian dies and then skip. The West Indies are a long way away and I could comfortably afford a bodyguard. I can see it would be a convenience if I went abroad as Lucas wants but I

58

simply don't feel inclined to oblige him. Would you?' he inquired.

'No, I don't think I would.'

'Then give him a discourteous answer.'

'Right. But I still think you'd better lie low for a bit.'

'I'm doing just that and I'll keep on doing it. You spoke of a bilker walking freely round London but I do nothing to make Rex Lucas lose face. I go nowhere near the gambling clubs, Rex Lucas's or anyone else's. In fact I've only been once in my life and that was the evening I lost my head. I know I do that far too easily, but when I'm thinking straight I'm not always stupid.'

'You don't strike me as stupid at all,' Paul said.

'That's kind of you but it's not quite true. You could truthfully say that I'm unpredictable. Men of my background often are. How's aunt Lilian, by the way?'

'Still dying.'

'She's been doing that for several years but she dies extremely hard. Greggs do.'

'A Gregg by marriage.'

'She's caught the habit. Does she still have the odd good day—bright as ever?'

'I haven't seen her for months.'

'Nor have I, come to that. Perhaps we might go together.'

'With pleasure.'

Paul hadn't meant to say it so pat. He'd deliver a message since he'd decided he must but he hadn't intended double harness. But he'd said it and he pulled out his diary. 'Would tomorrow week suit you?'

'Perfectly, thank you.'

'I'll be in London on the Thursday before so perhaps we could make an early start.'

'That'll be very pleasant indeed.'

Paul Martiny rose. 'It's been a pleasure to meet you.'

'It's been mutual,' Michael Horan said.

That evening Mike Horan went out to shop and in the street came face to face with the General. The General was looking tired and strained and he was evidently an embarrassed man.

'Good evening to you.'

'Good evening, sir.'

The General made a tiny gesture but the meaning of it was perfectly clear: he didn't wish to be addressed as 'Sir'. 'I'm going to ask a very great favour. You remember you said once you'd help if you could?'

'Anything I can do,' Mike said. He said it and he meant it sincerely.

'Then do you happen to know a decent doctor?' There was an emphasis on the adjective 'decent'. The General didn't mean a competent doctor.

'I know a doctor who's very broad-minded indeed.'

'It's my wife, you know—she's in very great pain. Her doctor has given her drugs of course, but they're less and less use and she's suffering terribly. I can't bear to watch her, I can't any more.' The General was suddenly, shatteringly human; he said in a very small voice to freeze the blood: 'Some doctors have ideas they shouldn't, they mix morals with the business of doctoring.'

'You needn't say more.'

'You're more than kind. Then this doctor of yours?'
'He has no religion.'
'Would he come to us if you asked him?'
'I think so.'
'Will you ask him?'
'At once.'
'I'm eternally grateful.'

Mike Horan went home and rang his doctor. He had thought of the General just once since his beating but of his doctor he hadn't thought at all.

Paul Martiny went back to his room to think. Two emotions were fighting to come out top. One was that he had liked Mike Horan. He was clearly, as he had said himself, unpredictable and probably worse, a hair-trigger man who'd go off if you shook him, but he was also at heart a rebel. So was Paul.

And the other emotion was simply annoyance. He had a powerful sense of family but Michael Horan was hardly within it. He had a duty to see his great aunt again but none in the world to take Horan with him. He was doing what he hated to do, involving himself for no logical reason. And there was something else he must do at once.

He rang up Rex Lucas to do it decisively. 'I gave your message.'
'I thank you for that. With success, I hope.'
'From your point of view with none whatever.'
'He turned down forty a week?'
'He'd have turned down a hundred.'
'I really think that's extremely foolish.'
'Listen,' Paul Martiny said; he had a message now to deliver himself. 'If you're thinking of further

violence, forget it. Remember that you told me things—'

'Which you'd take to the police who would no doubt listen. They'd listen to Mr Paul Martiny but they couldn't hang a handkerchief on your humble servant Rex Lucas, speaking.' The words had been edging quite close to offence but the voice was still as bland as silk. 'In any case I wasn't considering it. Events which I think you know nothing about have turned this matter inside out. I've no interest in putting more pressure on Horan till I'm sure that that pressure is worth my while.'

'I don't understand you.'

'I didn't intend it.'

Exceptionally Lucas was telling the truth: the situation was certainly inside out. No question now of compounding his debt into something which the law would recognize, far less of putting more pressure on Horan. For Fat George had been on the telephone and the news he had given the worst news possible. Not only were there indeed two Wills but the second had left Horan penniless.

Lucas wrote down the pros and cons on paper, a habit he had learnt from the English, then he put it away in his safe to mature. Fat George had noted the new heir's address and Lucas had despatched him to Norfolk. He was already convinced there was some sort of fiddle and local colour on the persons concerned would be a weapon which he wouldn't despise.

It wouldn't be his main one, though: he had already made his mind up on that. Twenty-two thousand English pounds was far from a sum to break his business, but Lucas had been born a Greek. This was a debt and he meant to collect it. The fact that if he made his collection it would cost a couple of men their lives was something he hadn't even considered. Good Greeks would always collect what was due to them.

He had rung the Exchange for Continental. 'Get me Palermo,' he said. 'It's in Sicily.' He gave them the number.

'We'll ring you back.'

When they did so the doctor's death had been certain.

7

Charlotte Tellier had motored up to see Clement. She didn't intend to stay at his Rectory, though she didn't suppose he was really the man to anticipate the mumbo jumbo. But now that she had him (she really *had* him!) she must behave with decorum and utter propriety, so she was staying with a friend in Norwich.

She turned the nose of her little car to the west, driving through the rich lush country, sugar beet and malting barley, sleek cattle lifting the opulent grass. She was thinking that what she'd been told was true, that Norfolk was the Texas of England. Most fields were twice the size of a southern, the farmhouses solid and clearly prosperous, real farms where men lived and worked hard at farming, not the surtax-avoidance toys of Kent. This country had once been the richest in England and even today it was still very rich. The enormous churches told her that, preposterous relics of dying altars. The really rich parishes built their towers square, those less prosperous built them round. The round sort were the cheaper to build. And every few miles she put behind her there was the mansion of some local magnate. In Norfolk they were as thick on the ground as apples under a smitten tree. Amazingly they were still mostly lived in. Somehow these people had kept their roots.

She had no ambition to own such a thing but she

was interested in Clement's Rectory. She remembered what she had thought before, that many Rectories were small country houses and with money could be made quite charming like those in the Essex commuting belt. Well, Mother had fixed the money side and all she need do was to suffer Clement. That wouldn't be easy, he was so *wet*, and he'd chosen to be very High Church in a diocese which was generally Low. He'd get no promotion this side of the ocean—she wasn't even sure he wished it. So she'd never be a bishop's wife but in these parts even a Rector's had standing. Not a great one perhaps, but established, accepted. Provided she minded her ps and qs she'd be asked to eat in those magnates' mansions. The more civilized of their various owners might even be pleased to see a new face.

... And if I find I can't take it I'll simply run. There isn't a thing he dare do to stop me and he can't afford to be other than generous. For once I'm on to something for nothing. That doesn't come often to women like me and when it does I'd be a fool not to grab it.

Even when the price was Clement.

Who was at this moment saying Mass, which he pronounced with a very long A—The Maass. Two parishes had been knocked into one, which meant that he had also two churches. In one of them he carried on (his parishioners' phrase and not his own) and in the other he held straight Anglican services. Not that it made a material difference. In the church where there were bells and smells the congregation was normally three, and in the other the score was a steady nine.

It was Sunday and he had asked her to lunch in

65

the Rectory of the parish of Strewdey. The other one had been long since sold off and in any case Charlotte's interest was Strewdey. He had told her in his pompous way that after he'd said his Maass he'd be preaching. Charlotte couldn't face that though soon she would have to, so she'd started late deliberately and a woman had let her into the Rectory.

He came in in a soup-spotted cassock and kissed her. He was a handsome man if you liked the type but his mouth was as soft and wet as a haddock.

'I'm sorry I didn't make the service. I got stuck behind an R.A.F. convoy.'

He didn't reject the apology but merely remarked that the R.A.F. was notoriously a nuisance locally. He spoke with self-conscious Christian charity but she could see that he was greatly offended.

'Would you care for a glass of sherry?'

'Yes please.' Charlotte had realized there wouldn't be gin and moreover the pubs on the way had been shut. Sunday morning in darkest Norfolk, she thought. I hope I can take it for two or three years. She sipped her sherry cautiously. It was Cyprus sherry and tasted of axle oil.

He saw her expression and misunderstood it. 'I needn't say that this isn't South African.'

'Some of them are rather good.'

'You cannot suppose that I'd buy from South Africa.'

She'd supposed just that since real sherry cost money.... Oh God, give me strength for a couple of years. It was down from two or three to two. What a pouf the man was, what a smell of sour wind, sitting in this preposterous Rectory, content among a

66

handful of faithful. She knew it was a College living, the sort they doled out to Good College Men. You rowed in the College boat, in the middle, then you took Orders which not many fancied. Your College, or rather Clement's College, had a tradition of rowing and also the Church. Naturally they'd looked after him.

The woman brought in a joint of beef, and Clement carved it, not very skilfully. There were soggy greens and roast potatoes which hadn't been drained from the fat they'd been cooked in. Clement opened a bottle of grocer's claret. 'A little celebration,' he said.

The wine, never good, was by now half vinegar, and Charlotte Tellier drank some reluctantly. But the Reverend Clement appeared to enjoy it. It certainly relaxed his manner from the stuffiness with which he'd greeted her. 'I've been thinking,' he said.

'Oh yes? About what?'

But she had guessed what would be coming again, the business of aunt Lilian's money, and a very great bore that was bound to be—his principles and his ridiculous conscience. But though these would bore Miss Tellier stiff they no longer frightened her quite so sharply. She'd have agreed that at one time they'd really scared her, that talk of division, of sharing fairly. She had feared that he might be serious, that some action might lie below the froth. Now she was fairly sure it wouldn't. It was one thing to talk about sacred trusts, quite another when you found yourself possessed of great wealth which you owned un-challengeably. Property had a curious virtue, not in theory but in observable fact. When you had it you changed your ideas remarkably.

And her mother, when approached with these worries, had laughed and had told her a little story. Before she'd established her Home for the Elderly she'd been a matron in a well-known clinic, and one day they'd brought in a rabid Leftie who was also engaged to a rich man's son. His family hadn't liked the affair but the son had been entirely besotted, so they'd behaved with intelligence, even with cunning. The mother had shown her strong disapproval, but the father had been experienced, and one day he'd come with a fine string of pearls. And what does Miss Leftie do with these baubles? Does she sell them and give the proceeds to Oxfam? No, she puts them on and gloats for a month. She wears them day and night unceasingly and you can't get them off her, not even anaesthetized. She starts reading the *Daily Telegraph*, and when her old friends call she sends them away.

Charlotte had laughed at the tale politely, but she guessed that it was probably true and it had comforted her in her private doubt. So she was letting this idiot talk his head off, how he'd see that all the family were looked after according to varying needs, then give something to some missionaries who were wrecking the ancestral habits of a perfectly healthy tribe of pagans. Finally he would set up a Trust for the benefit of poor Bangladeshis. Where old Gregg had so doubtfully made his fortune.

She let him drivel all through luncheon.

Afterwards they sat in his poky study. Clement had sat down too heavily in a chair which she at once decided should be one of the very first things to go. She could see that he wasn't drunk, or not properly,

68

but he'd drunk most of a bottle he wasn't accustomed to, and what he really wanted was simply sleep.... This man is with his official fiancée and though I say it myself she's not unattractive. And all he wants is to get his feet up. All right, I won't stop him.

She rose and smiled. 'I expect you've got Sunday School later.'

'I have. It's kind of you to think of it.'

It's kind of me, she thought. Oh hell. 'I'll see you next week, then. Down at Westercombe. My mother is looking forward to meeting you.'

She wasn't but she'd played ball at once.... But a clergyman! And a Spike at that.

'Do you think I ought to sleep in your house?'

'I don't see why not with Mother there.'

'Perhaps an inn would be better.'

An inn. In Westercombe.

'Just as you fancy. I'll book you a room.'

'And I'll have to leave on Saturday evening. Sunday is my heaviest day.'

Heaviest day, indeed. A sinecure.

He took her arm to her little car in the drive, opening the door politely. 'Till Friday,' Clement Melsome said. For a moment she thought he would stand back and wave but some sense of what would be proper seized him. He put his head through the window and kissed her chastely.

It was still like kissing a filleted haddock. Even the smell was not so different.

She waved back since it was the thing to do, but she'd send him to a competent dentist.

Fat George arrived in the village of Strewdey on

the Sunday morning of Charlotte's visit. He was tired and thirsty and went to the pub, discovering it was still firmly shut. He remembered what day of the week it was: this was something to do with the hours of church services and he cursed church services hard and heartily. When the pub at last opened he went to the bar. Mysteriously four evident locals were already inside and drinking mild though Fat George had been a queue of one. He ordered two pints of bitter and drank them. The landlord distantly declined one himself.

Fat George was a little put out by this. He didn't use village pubs very often, but by everything he'd ever read they were places where you picked up the gossip. Yet when he had asked the way to the Rectory the landlord had simply waved a hand, and the locals were somewhat self-consciously sunk in a complicated game of shove-ha'penny. The atmosphere wasn't exactly hostile but nor was it in any way welcoming.

As it happened Fat George had been unlucky. His clothes and his car outside said 'London', and at this moment, in the village of Strewdey, London was a dirty word. For a month ago men had come in cars and marched to Melsome's other church, the one whereat, by local consensus, he behaved like a lunatic Jesuit and worse. They'd had banners painted in bold black letters.

DOWN WITH THE POPE

NO COMPROMISE OF THE PROTESTANT FAITH

They hadn't been looking for open trouble, they hadn't thrown stones or caused a disturbance, but they'd picketed Clement Melsome's church, and when he came out in a smart biretta they had booed him and made rude remarks. He'd escaped in his car but they had had theirs, and they'd followed him to his Rectory lawn. Melsome had summoned the police.

They had come. Or rather a single constable came. In this part of Norfolk there were still village policemen and this autocrat had not been pleased that his Sunday peace had been roughly disturbed. He had made his displeasure extremely plain and no villager wished to incur it again. So Fat George, who was clearly a man from London, was treated with a massive reserve.... Hadn't he asked for the Rectory? Yes. And why should any sane man do that? He didn't look the sort of man who'd be one of the Reverend's curious friends, and anyway it was Sunday morning when even clergymen of the Established Church were by Statute required to do some work.

So Fat George drank his beer and went on to the Rectory. He didn't have any plan of action but Rex Lucas had told him that trifles were relevant and by watching he could absorb the aura. After lunch Mr Melsome might take a stroll, and Fat George had brought his field-glasses with him.

He parked in a neighbouring wood and walked, slipping through the Rectory's policies till he was opposite to the open front door. He noticed it needed a coat of paint, then he hid behind a rhododendron. There was a car in the crumbling drive outside.

After half an hour George was bored and stiff but he couldn't return quite empty-handed. At the least he must have sight of this Melsome. Fat George let a grunt of irritation but stayed determinedly behind his shrub.

And at quarter past two two people came out, a man in a cassock, a girl beside him. The man was tall and thin and nondescript and he was holding the arm of the girl he walked with. Fat George put his glasses up and swallowed. He knew this girl, it was Charlotte Tellier, the bird he'd stood up when he'd gone to Westercombe. He adjusted the glasses and stared again. She was wearing an engagement ring which she hadn't been when he'd propositioned her. The man handed her into her car and kissed her. The car drove away and the girl waved back. Fat George allowed it a handsome headstart, then he whipped up a lumbering trot to the wood. For now he had red hot news, a scoop.

He didn't stop on the way to telephone Lucas: Lucas would see him at any time, at any place with news like this. Fat George drove straight to his private house.

'You're disturbing a party. I hope it's worth it.'

'This is worth more than any party. There's a woman called Miss Charlotte Tellier. I know her because I was trying to lay her. Her mother keeps the Home for the Elderly where old Lady Gregg is going to die. And this woman was calling on Clement Melsome. I think that she's now engaged to him. To the Melsome who's now Lady Gregg's new heir. Or he is under that second Will.'

Rex Lucas didn't need to consider; he had taken it in as Fat George spoke it. 'I follow,' he said. 'Very smart indeed.'

... In the matter of inheriting property the English rule was Anything Goes.

Rex Lucas didn't go back to his party. He knew now

what sort of racket this was. It was a family racket, the most savage of all.

He wasn't surprised and far from shocked, for in spite of what Paul Martiny had told him he was sure that he understood the English. Intrigue was in his blood and bowels, the double cross was the natural air he breathed, but he also had a fastidious mind which was offended by the English habit of wrapping everything up in flannel. In their internal affairs, which they grossly mismanaged, they had phrases like welfare and social justice, and in international politics they shied from the naked face of power. They were drunk with abstractions, clearly decadent, but in one last affair they were still quite ruthless and that was in inheriting property. Amongst the people who had such a thing to pass on a hardened criminal would have looked an innocent.

'It's a jungle,' he said aloud, 'a jungle.' He'd been convinced before that the jungle existed—what Fat George had discovered at Heale-Mann's office had made that as certain as anything could be—but this further report from a village in Norfolk had completed the picture and rounded it out. Now he knew the animals who were stalking their good red meat in the undergrowth: a woman who kept a Home for the Elderly where another of ninety was easy prey, her daughter who was engaged to a clergyman, a solicitor in a country practice and the doctor who'd witnessed the new Will with him, the Will which put Horan out, the clergyman in.

Very pretty. Very clever indeed.

But happily it wasn't quite watertight, not with a woman of over ninety, and the potential flaws which might sink the ship were these witnesses who, if the Will were challenged, would have to convince a sceptical judge that the old lady had been fit to make it. And of the two the doctor had clearly come first.

Rex Lucas was pleased he had rung to Palermo. The man who had answered was known simply as Enzo, for his eminence in his dangerous trade made any other name superfluous. He was as different from that stooge Fat George as any two men could possibly be.

Which reminded Lucas—he owed Fat George money. Twenty a day he had promised him, which he thought generous for easy work in the country, and also what he'd called proper expenses. Which hadn't been defined. That was excellent. Fat George was a Cypriot, Rex Lucas a mainlander. Both of them were therefore Greeks and neither to be in any way blamed if he tried to cheat the other shamelessly.

More important he had heard again from the man who had come over from Sicily. Lucas had put his proposition, and Enzo, after due thought, had accepted.... So the doctor first? That's a matter for you.

And now he had reported from Westercombe. He hadn't said much, he seldom did; he was remarkably free of Latin bombast. He had simply got on with his job, which was killing. In any case he'd be calling tomorrow, when they'd quietly discuss his second duty. That second duty was Gilbert Heale-Mann, Solicitor, Commissioner for Oaths, and witness to inconvenient Testaments.

8

Enzo was calling at ten o'clock and Rex Lucas had prepared himself carefully. He took from his safe the paper he'd written and read it again with a lively pleasure. When he'd written it he had known from Fat George that a second Will in fact existed, but Fat George had not yet visited Strewdey and the story had been incomplete. Reading this paper a second time Rex Lucas, who wasn't modest, was gratified. He thought himself extremely farsighted. Against the first two paragraphs he wrote in red pencil 'Hypothesis confirmed' and left them. It was the third which still was relevant, still the guts and the hearts of what had to be done.

3. Lady Gregg cannot be under any Order from the Court of Protection or anything similar. If she were no solicitor, not even a bent one, would dare put another Will before her. It follows that the validity of the new one depends on her state of mind when she made it. The witnesses were carefully chosen, a solicitor of good standing locally, and, even more important, her doctor. But for these two the Will would be vulnerable. It could probably be challenged successfully.

Rex Lucas read this again, smiling happily.... *But for these two the Will would be vulnerable.* He was delighted he hadn't held his hand and waited till the whole picture was clearer but had rung to Palermo at once. He'd saved time.

Rex Lucas shared with Paul Martiny a very poor opinion of lawyers and at no time had he even considered the dry dust and expense of legal advice. If he took this story to any lawyer he'd be bound to wonder how he'd obtained it, and if he suppressed the names and his own real interest, presenting a hypothetical case, the lawyer might well decline to advise. Even if he agreed to do so he would probably talk about Counsel's Opinion. Rex Lucas knew perfectly well what that meant. It was almost the hardest thing in the World to get Counsel to say: 'I think you'll win.' If he did and you didn't he lost much face and his livelihood depended on face. And he'd hardly ever say: 'You'll lose' because if he said that he lost a Brief. So what you got was a conducted tour round the precedents and recent cases.... In Smith and Jones the Court decided, but in the Appeal Court it went the other way. But only by a majority, so of course one cannot be wholly sure. Rex Lucas despised this charade wholeheartedly. It was more practical and in the end cost less money to ring up a man like Enzo in Sicily.

No doubt there were certain risks: he'd accepted them. His principle was to have strings on people, on Fat George whom he held by the shortest hairs, on two croupiers who'd been run out of France, on his frighteners and his strongarms too, on the smooth young man whom he used as a messenger. But on Enzo, he had no string whatever. Enzo in his own harsh trade was every bit as successful as Lucas. That couldn't be helped, he needed Enzo. He'd decided that some days ago, and on what Fat George had brought back from Strewdey it was clear he now needed him more than ever.

Enzo was now announced and came in. He was indeed as different from Fat George as any man could possibly be. In Sicily titles were six for ten lire and Enzo seldom used his own, but the fact that he didn't hang out his label in no way diminished his cool distinction. He was tall and thin, bought his clothes in London, and by now he was very comfortably off. Enzo didn't need to kill for money but chose his jobs with a cold fastidiousness. If they appealed to his sense of craftsmanship, almost to his sense of art, he would take them for a swingeing fee but for money alone wouldn't raise a hand. He said to Rex Lucas, his manner reflective:

'This killing is a curious business. Any fool can kill a man provided he will accept two conditions. The first is that it will look like a killing and the second is that he will have to run. I've done that before when I was younger and had to, but by now it doesn't appeal any more. In any case I never had bloodlust. The good killing must leave a margin of doubt. Could this in fact be no more than an accident? The really artistic killing goes further. It looks like an accident outright.' Enzo accepted a glass of champagne. 'It follows that if you agree to these standards you must also agree to the limits they put on you. You cannot just go out and shoot, you're obliged to wait for an opportunity.'

'I gather from the fact that you've called that you didn't wait long to deal with that doctor.'

Enzo said modestly: 'There I was lucky. An elderly man walks alone on a cliff. There was a fence which I could see was suspect. So I didn't throw him over it, I pushed him through and left it broken.'

Rex Lucas nodded appreciation. He was a Greek and Enzo Sicilian but both of them were Mediterraneans, both could appreciate acts of art. And if such acts earned good money too the Mediterranean soul was happy.

But Enzo had begun to talk again. 'Though there's one thing which still puzzles me.'

'Tell me,' Rex Lucas said. He meant it. You couldn't hire a man of Enzo's calibre and simply say: 'Kill X and Y for me.' He would want to know the reasons behind it, for the reasons, your private motives for killing, were relevant to the risks he'd be running. He was a long way by now from a gun for hire.

'You gave me the background—I think I followed it. A man owes you twenty-two thousand pounds. He can't pay it but he is also an heir; he's the heir under an old lady's Will. But some parties whom you didn't mention—you didn't name them because it wasn't necessary—have cooked up another Will instead which has cut out the present heir completely and with it your hopes of getting paid. The old lady is very old indeed, so old that she's not above suspicion that she doesn't know what she'd really be signing, so to make a new Will stand up at all it would have to be very carefully witnessed. The witnesses who were involved in this case were her doctor and her new solicitor. Remove them and the Will won't stand up, or rather it may not stand up if challenged.'

'Correct,' Lucas said. 'That's entirely correct.'

'Then the thing which still puzzles me is this. I may

be a very ignorant man, but why kill two men when one would do?'

'I don't think I follow.'

'Then why not kill the new beneficiary, the man who will probably scoop the pool if the witnesses to the second Will live?'

'Because that wouldn't restore the first Will. You can do that by only one way I know, which is to show that the second Will was invalid—either that it was made under pressure or else that the aged party who made it was past knowing what she was really doing. I don't say this would be quite impossible if these carefully chosen witnesses lived; I do say that without this doctor and lawyer it's going to be a great deal easier.'

Enzo thought it over carefully. 'I see. So we put them out of the way. That's your business. But then someone must challenge the second Will?'

'Exactly so.'

'And who will that be?'

'The beneficiary under the first of course.'

'The man who owes you this money?'

'Yes.'

'And suppose he doesn't.'

'He has an interest in doing so.'

'You can never be sure in a country like England. They're a totally incomprehensible people.'

'If he doesn't,' Rex said, 'I believe I can make him. Some very unpleasant things could still happen.'

'That I don't doubt. I wish you well.' Enzo said it though he didn't like Lucas.

'And the matter outstanding?' Rex Lucas asked.

'You mean the lawyer who also witnessed the Will?'

'This corrupt or at best corrupted lawyer.'

'That may take a little time.'

'I'd be obliged if you could make it a short one.'

'I told you the terms—I don't kill blindly.'

'And talking of terms I should like to confirm them. I think we said five thousand pounds. Two thousand when the first one died and the other three when you got the second.'

'That is correct,' Enzo said. He was shaken. This wasn't the sort of uncouth language which was used between two civilized men.

Lucas handed across two hundred tenners which Enzo accepted with half a bow. Secretly he was quietly amused. He knew all about Lucas's reputation, that he would twist you if he could on principle—it was a reflex, really, he couldn't help it—but Enzo was also wholly confident that his own reputation would make that unlikely. He was not only eminent in his difficult trade, he was Sicilian and known to be ruthless, not a man to accept a double cross helplessly. And apparently he'd been perfectly right for here was the first instalment as promised. So Enzo put the money away and listened again to Lucas talking.

'We were discussing the timing.'

'So we were. It depends on what chances this lawyer offers me.'

'Ten days, would you say?'

'I would hope rather less.'

Enzo would have agreed very willingly that again he'd had more than normal good fortune. Rex Lucas had suggested ten days and Enzo had in turn hoped for less. Now it was going to be notably less, a matter of a mere five days. This one wouldn't be another classic, something which stayed looking an accident, but for a moment it would do just that and that moment ensured a certain getaway.

So it was fortunate that Sir Duncan Gregg's mansion was being razed as the useless eyesore it was, and it was fortunate that Gilbert Heale-Mann, when he wasn't doing something disgraceful, was conscientious in his clients' interests. Old Lady Gregg was one of those clients, and every Saturday morning, wet or fine, he went out to check up on the demolition. Very valuable things could be found in a wrecking, and not every man who worked on a building site was as honest as perhaps he might be. The Paddys were the worst of all.

It was a job against time and men would be working, even on a Saturday morning, but Enzo wasn't worried by that. Their first thought would be to help the injured and he'd be away before any other occurred to them.

And above all it was lucky he'd served in the war. It hadn't been a distinguished service. Enzo was a Sicilian and like all his race a clear-headed realist. He'd surrendered at the first opportunity, choosing British troops to surrender to. He had heard the Free French could be rough with prisoners.

So he'd spent most of his war as a well-fed prisoner but he'd also learnt to drive tracked vehicles. He moved his hands in recollection.... Push on the left lever, pull the right. That meant braking the left track, speeding the other. Naturally the vehicle moved

81

to the left. He had made a recce late one night. The house inside was by now a shell but the walls were still standing, including the front one. In the sea of mud around the house was a single dry spot for parking cars, and duckboards led away from it directly to the impressive front door.

Enzo had also inspected the crane. The engine looked simple enough to start. He couldn't have handled a grader with shovels, the men who did that more than earned their money, but a simple crane on a pair of tracks was well within his modest competence. And he needn't do any lifting or lowering. All the jib carried was a ball and two wires. One suspended the demolition ball, the other one wound it back to the ready. Then you slipped a catch and the ball went away. It went away and it knocked a wall down.

Enzo thought the whole device a barbarity. In Sicily they still did it with mattocks and saved the bricks to build again. Barbarous then, but it was also convenient.

For a moment he thought of ringing Lucas, but he shrugged and decided he wouldn't do so. Lucas would simply think he was boasting, so better to wait till the job was done. Then he'd collect his three thousand happily, the more so since he disliked Rex Lucas. Twenty-two thousand was the debt which was owed him, and a rich man who'd pay five to get back that could only be a Greek. He detested them.

The Paddy was drinking whisky and boasting and Enzo was buying a lot of whisky. 'It's a piece of cake,' the Paddy was saying, 'as easy as kiss your arse or easier. We come over here and we swindle the natives. They don't even know that we hate their guts. All

82

you have to do is a little work, something they won't do themselves. I work in the building trade—demolitions.'

'And what do you do?'

'I drive a crane. I make a lot of money too, I tell you that since I don't think you're English. I made even more when we worked the lump, but the British have got round to that one. Now you have to have a Green Card to fix that. God damn the Brits but I'll take their money. With overtime I take a lot of it.'

Enzo bought the Paddy another drink, paying cash at the squalid public bar where he'd discovered that this savage drank. Secretly he felt mildly sick. Like most Latins he despised the Celt and as a man of achievement he hated boasting. And he had guessed why this pig was getting drunk. He didn't really need the stuff, what he really wanted was something quite different, but that would be quite a serious sin, whereas drunkenness rated a hundred *Aves*. A good Catholic, Enzo was quietly scandalized. Good God, were their priests uncivilized too? It was supposed to be a Catholic country but its sexual *mores* were shamefully Protestant. Enzo owned several prosperous brothels which his confessor, though he doubtless deplored them, regarded with Mediterranean tolerance. But Enzo needed this man or at least his absence.

'Will you have another drink?' he asked.

'You're very kind. I'll take a whisky.' It was the eighth or ninth and the Paddy was going. Enzo had been pouring his own in a fern. 'I must go to the john,' the Paddy said.

'I'll wait for you.'

83

'I can see you're not English.'

While the Paddy was drunkenly splashing his trousers Enzo quietly doctored his waiting drink. It wasn't a knock-out—quite to the contrary. But the Paddy wouldn't be working next morning.

When the Paddy came back Enzo had gone. The Paddy sighed; he had liked him—a gentleman.

The foreman had been suspicious at first. 'You're Irish too?' he had asked.

'I am not.'

'You don't talk quite English.'

'I'm not that either.'

'But you're a friend of this man who you say has gone sick?'

'How otherwise should I know he was ill? I told him that I could drive so he sent me.'

The foreman was on the horns and knew it. There was only one crane and one man to drive it. It was a contract job and a Saturday morning. His firm stood to lose a full morning's work and for that he would be unjustly blamed. 'Then show me your Union card,' he said.

Enzo hadn't thought of that one; he stared. 'I left it at home,' he said at last.

The foreman hesitated again but finally took it. 'I'll chance it for once—it's regular rates. Regular rates and a half for Saturday. Now show me you can do what you say.'

They walked to the crane and Enzo started the engine, warming it before he used it. Then he put a track in gear and moved it. It was easier than he'd dared to hope.

'Okay, you can have her. Now listen to me. You see that door with a wall both sides? It looks valuable but in fact it's rubbish—not worth the labour of taking it out. I want the whole side broken up. Think you can do it?'

'I think I can.'

Enzo checked on the ball at the end of its wire; it was already wound back and he checked the release catch. It was all quite straightforward. His confidence rose.

He began to drive the crane to position, rather relishing that he did so competently. He could see that a family car had arrived. A man in later middle life was climbing out a little stiffly. Enzo noticed he wasn't wearing boots and the ground round the site would be almost impassable. He'd have to go along the duckboards; he'd have to go past the front door; he'd had it.

... All according to plan. My lucky plan.

Enzo made a final adjustment and waited. The man had twenty paces to go and at the nineteenth Enzo would pull the release.

... Seventeen, eighteen, nineteen. Pull.

The ball went away and destroyed the door. It smashed it yards into the shell of the house. With it it took what was left of Heale-Mann.

When the foreman got to the crane again Enzo had reached his car and was moving.

9

It was two hundred miles from London to Westercombe, and Paul, as he'd arranged with Mike Horan,
started that Friday morning early. He never thought
of a car as a symbol of status but his own, though
unostentatious, was fast. They drove in an almost
total silence and Paul Martiny was grateful for it.
He knew the road and Horan didn't, so Mike Horan
didn't fuss with maps, far less back-seat drive or chatter
idly. Occasionally he smoked or nodded. He was in
fact the text-book passenger.

This was partly because he drove himself and partly
because he was feeling sad. Not for himself or for
Lilian Gregg who he didn't believe would wish to live
longer in a world in which she was now an anachron-
ism, but for the General who lived in the flat above
him and had once saved him from a military prison.
Normally he was a dapper old boy—bowler hat, rolled
umbrella and Greenjackets tie—but now he was showing the signs of age. A lifetime's discipline still held
him firmly; he was clean and shaven and perfectly
tidy, but the spring had gone out of his step, he looked
harassed. He always took his hat off politely—the
white lining was spotless—but the gesture had lost
its usual panache.

Mike had known about the General's wife even
before the General's request to him. She had had two
operations already and he'd heard that a third was

now out of the question. He wasn't worried for her since he'd never met her but he was worried for a man he admired.

On the rare stretches where he needn't concentrate Paul Martiny was also thinking—of Horan. He was sitting there quiet and self-possessed but his history held wicked flashes of violence which had all been disproportionate, ill-judged in their timing and always harming him. As he'd said himself he was quite unpredictable. Martiny chanced a glance at him sideways. He was dark and long-headed, his eyes were fine. Had he Spanish blood? It was perfectly possible. There were parts of the country his father had come from where such blood was much more than a peasant tradition. If he had it would explain a great deal, the flares of uncontrollable temper, the confident unaffected manner, above all things the prickly self-respect.

Martiny returned to the road and his driving. All this was the purest speculation and he didn't need to speculate to know that he very much liked Mike Horan. He would do a very great deal to help him and do it without reward and gladly.

As they drew into Westercombe Martiny asked: 'Where do you stay when you visit aunt Lilian?'

'I go to *The Bull* but it's only two stars.'

'I've been using *The Imperial*—four stars and pretty flashy too. I'd be glad of a change so we'll go to *The Bull*.'

They checked in and left their bags, freshened up. Martiny knocked at Mike Horan's door. 'It's a quarter to twelve so it's lunch or aunt Lilian.'

'If it's all right with you I'd rather go to her first.

In the afternoon she mostly sleeps and in the evening she isn't normally with you.'

'How long since you saw her last?'

'Two months, I'd say.'

'You've done better than I have.'

They got into the car again and drove to Mrs Tellier's *The Laurels*. It was a late Victorian seaside villa, the quintessential house of its time, superlatively built but ugly, almost a caricature of its type—the shrubs in the garden, the inescapable monkey-puzzle. The porch had stained glass on either side and outside in the semi-circular drive was a discreet little board which said:

HOME FOR THE ELDERLY

In a corner, more discreetly still, in a gothic script which made Martiny wince, was:

Matron. Mrs Dorothy Tellier

They rang the bell and she opened the door herself. Martiny had rung her the evening before. 'Come in, please,' she said but quite without welcome. They followed her to her sitting-room and the three of them sat down together. This was normal procedure, she always did it, whether for Martiny or Horan.

'Would you care for a cup of coffee?'

'No thank you.'

Paul had spoken at once without waiting for Horan. He was a man who trusted his instincts utterly and at this moment they were signalling furiously. He wanted to see what this woman did next, not sit pointlessly sipping at nasty coffee.

There was something here which wasn't quite right.

She obliged his wish for action immediately. 'I'm

afraid you can't see your aunt today.'

'Why ever not?' It was Horan now.

'Because,' she said coldly, 'the doctor says so.'

'I rang you last night and you didn't mention it.' Martiny was smoother but just as angry.

'There's no need to be nasty,' Mrs Tellier said.

They were Paul Martiny's unfavourite words, the basilisk phrase of a vulgar woman. Cross this type in any way whatever and out came at once: 'There's no need to be nasty.' An attempt to wrong foot you? Perhaps it was. But it also told you a lot of the speaker.

There was something much more than odd going on.

Mike Horan had started to speak again but Paul held his hand up and stopped him dead. He said as he rose:

'I accept what you say but we'll call tomorrow.'

'I can make you no promises.'

'Nor do I ask them.'

'She may well be a good deal worse tomorrow.'

'Or conceivably she may well be better.' Paul had made up his mind what he meant to do. There wasn't any point in arguing, far less in accepting the evident risk that Mike Horan would lose his explosive temper. If Horan did that he would really wrong foot them.

Mrs Tellier led them back through the corridor, sweeping the front door open dismissively. She was clearly in a vicious temper; she would have loved to raise her foot but didn't dare.

So she opened the door and stood aside, glowering. Unexpectedly she shut it again for a car had drawn up in the little drive and a man and a woman were

89

climbing out. Charlotte had been to the town to meet Clement. The fools, her mother thought, the blundering fools. They had said after lunch and here they were, arriving openly under the enemy's eyes. She had very much rather they hadn't done so. Neither of these two men was a fool. At the least there must now be some introductions and Mrs Tellier would have liked to avoid them.

But she couldn't hustle them out through the kitchen door, she'd have to play it by ear and watch what happened. Her moment of indecision passed and she reopened the door as her daughter arrived at it. She put on her very best mother's smile and kissed Charlotte with apparent affection. To Clement Melsome she said:

'I'm delighted to see you.'

What happened then surprised her greatly for in the hall, still behind her, Paul Martiny spoke:

'Hullo Charlotte. How are you?'

'Hullo Paul. You look well.'

Mrs Tellier was distinctly put out. She had faced the fact that it wasn't acceptable to have four people at a door at a time without some sociable word of introduction. Moreover Charlotte was her only daughter and Clement her future son-in-law. These facts were bound to come out in time but she would have greatly preferred that that time were not now. To Mike Horan she had planned an injury and Martiny she had never liked; he looked the sort who wouldn't go quietly and indeed he had just established it. All that she'd accepted but not this event. She hadn't known Charlotte had met Paul Martiny; she said in a voice which she hoped was neutral:

'I didn't know you'd met already.'

Charlotte smiled sweetly. 'We met in London.'

'I see.' Mrs Dorothy Tellier frowned. It might have meant just 'I see' or it mightn't.

Charlotte took over: her manners were better. 'Good morning, Mr Horan.'

'Good morning.'

Dorothy Tellier was losing control; she said awkwardly:

'So you know him too?'

'Not very well, I'm afraid. We're just neighbours.' Charlotte Tellier turned to the man behind her. He wore a dog collar in the Roman style, only the front two inches showing. 'My fiancé, Clement Melsome,' she said. Paul Martiny had noticed her ring already.

Clement Melsome didn't speak but bowed. Paul Martiny said: 'Congratulations.'

Melsome gave him a very clerical smile. 'Thank you. That's very kind indeed.' He'd begun to squeak which he did in embarrassment. He knew Paul had saved him once. He was sweating.

These exchanges, such as they were, now ended and Dorothy Tellier stood aside. Paul guessed that she would gladly have murdered him but he went past her calmly with Michael Horan. 'Till tomorrow,' he said to the furious woman.

She'd recovered a little. 'If the doctor permits it.'

'I've a feeling that he's going to permit it.'

In the car driving back Paul said to Horan: 'What do you make of that?'

'I don't like it.'

'Any particular reason?'

'No reason.'

'I know what you mean. I feel the same. One needn't be ashamed of feelings.'

'Very well then, I think there's something fishy.'

'And fish when it isn't fresh can smell. Would you care to put a name to the stink?'

Mike Horan thought it over carefully. 'Corruption,' he said at last.

'Not quite. The word I had thought of myself was "perfidy".'

'You mean there's some fiddle?'

'A pretty big one.'

They drove on for a moment in total silence. Paul Martiny broke it. 'We've still time for lunch.'

'Please have it alone, I've lost my appetite.'

'We seem to think and feel alike. If I ate just now I'd bring it up. I could use a drink, though.'

'And so could I.'

On the third gin Paul Martiny said: 'I'm going to call her bluff and call it now.'

'Her story about the doctor, you mean? You felt she was lying?'

'I did.'

'So did I, though I couldn't tell you why.'

'Then I know the name of her doctor. I'll ring him.'

He was back in five minutes and walking fast. 'Her doctor has been dead two days. He fell off a cliff through a broken fence and by now they will have scraped up the pieces. It'll all be in the local paper. It comes out tomorrow. I mean to buy it.'

Mike Horan said: 'You look different—uneasy.'

'That puts it a little high. But it's odd.'

'It could be a coincidence.'

'Certainly. But coincidences make my thumbs itch.'

Paul Martiny sat down with his drink, considering, for the local paper would tell him nothing. An accident to a well-liked doctor would be deplorable and therefore deplored but there was unlikely to be anything else. Already a local councillor would be gunning for some wretched official, one responsible for fences and lighting, but the doctor would have no obvious enemies and the town would accept the facts as they stood.

But if the Telliers were brewing something, and Paul was perfectly sure they were doing just that, the most likely field was old Lilian's Will. Paul frowned for he'd had experience of Wills. There'd been that matter of his distant kinsman, the tiresomely modern bishop of Basingstoke. He liked to be called Bill Basingstoke and he was pushful and very far to the Left. He had also double-crossed an uncle. The old man had left him a large sum of money and also named him as his sole executor. And just before this uncle had died he had written to the bishop, his heir. He had asked that the sum of ten thousand pounds (Bill Basingstoke would get nearer ninety) be given to a bastard daughter, but though the letter had been properly signed it was only a request, unwitnessed. It hadn't therefore been a formal codicil and Bill Basingstoke had blandly ignored it. There'd been some talk of a suit in the courts of law but the advice had been it could hardly succeed, or only at prohibitive cost, for Bill Basingstoke who was rich already would appeal and go on appealing grimly. In the end the bishop had taken the lot. Paul Martiny simply thought him greedy, though you could hardly be anything other than that and a Left Wing ambitious bishop too.

Paul sighed again; he hated dishonour. Helping criminals was entirely illegal but it left his private ethos unscathed. He didn't hate the way money was mostly made, he hated the way it was passed after death, the grasping, the trickery, family feuds. He hadn't heard Rex Lucas's dictum that in matters of inheriting property the English rule was Anything Goes, but he would in fact have put it higher. When it came to carving a dead man up quite decent people behaved like animals.

'We're going back to *The Laurels* tomorrow morning.'

'She'll only throw us out again.'

'I do not think she will throw us out.'

'You mean to push her face in then?' Mike Horan would clearly have joined in the action.

'Not push her face in—call her bluff. That doctor of hers died two days ago so we can't find out if he gave that order that aunt Lilian was too ill for visitors. But we can call in another doctor to see her, a big name from London to scare madam severely, particularly if she's been telling a lie and keeping us out for some private motive.'

'You still think there's something cooking there?'

'And I'm perfectly sure that it's something disgraceful. I can't prove a thing but I suspect it's a Will-fiddle.'

'You could very well be right at that.' Mike Horan reflected, then put the question. 'And supposing she chooses to call *your* bluff?'

'It isn't a bluff, I know just such a doctor. To come

at my call would be unprofessional but he's got very good reasons to do me a favour.'

'That'll all take time,' Mike Horan objected.

'If she's difficult I've another card, and one we can bang down at once. Aunt Lilian may or may not be that sick, but the Tellier is refusing entry to perfectly authentic relations. Unless she can show there's a doctor behind her there are various legal games we can play and some of them are rather tough. I don't like lawyers but I know how to use them.'

Mike Horan looked at Martiny thoughtfully. 'I'm very glad you're not my enemy.'

10

As the two men drove back to *The Laurels* next
morning Mike Horan looked sideways at Paul
Martiny, deciding that his courteous manner hid a
determined and very tough man indeed and one he
could respect and trust. The respect sprang from the
determination, not evident at first, clear now, but
the trust came from instinct, not observation. For why
should a man like Paul Martiny go out of his way
to help such as Mike Horan? With nine men in ten
the answer was simple: he wouldn't in fact be helping
him, he'd have designs on aunt Lilian's money himself. The thought was a long way from innocent; it
had occurred to him but he'd dismissed it at once.
Paul Martiny wasn't that sort of man. His motives for
offering help might be strange; they weren't the
dogooder's passion for what he thought proper, there
was no hint of the abrasive patronage of the man
who helped lame dogs over their stiles. For an instant
Mike Horan touched the truth. Perhaps this man who
sat beside him, this apparently establishment figure,
had a secret contempt for the world he'd been born in.
If so he concealed it since needs he must.

Mike Horan let his breath out softly. Paul Martiny's
motives were speculation but also they were now
irrelevant; what mattered was that help had been
offered, that he could accept it without the least
reservation. Paul Martiny had all the money he
needed, and Horan was entirely confident that he

hadn't an interest in grabbing more. You could trust him and Mike Horan did.

For his part Paul wasn't consciously thinking but letting his mind play around old aunt Lilian. The scenes came up, then faded away, with the maddening inconsequence of a thriller on commercial telly. He hadn't been born when she'd married Gregg, but later his mother had told him the story. There hadn't been quite a family rumpus but the elders had withheld approval. Duncan had been dark and dour, a lowland Scot with his way to make. Lilian, Paul Martiny gathered, had loved him at sight and had married him quickly, and from the picture of the world of those times, the flash-backs which his mother had shown him, Paul hadn't a doubt she had acted wisely. Far better a lowland Scot on the make than officers fingering lush dundrearies, the mashers (was that the word?) and society. And Lilian had always been very strong-willed, it was one of the reasons Paul had always admired her. It was a pity she'd never borne Duncan children, for if she had aunt Lilian's story—he corrected himself: the lady's career—might well have been completely orthodox. Orthodox and a great deal less interesting.

So Gregg had carried her off to Calcutta, to his job in one of the Managing Agents. The picture was rather clearer now for Martiny had read much about India. These great merchant houses in Bombay and Madras, above all the three or four in Calcutta, had in effect controlled Imperial India, the sinews of commercial power behind the tinsel of the Raj at its summit. In effect no doubt, but not in appearance.... Viceregal Lodge or a Governor's Bodyguard. Sikhs with beards wound round strings and improbable uniforms, impressive as ceremonial troops, often treacherous as fighting soldiers.

How aunt Lilian would have laughed at it all, a second-class country for a second-class people, its formality and the rigid precedence. The last must have made her laugh loudest of all, for there was a book bound in blue which gave everyone's standing, something respected by most officials and sacred to every official's wife. For aunt Lilian had a private precedence, tiny but officially recognized, so she processed into dinner before her husband, before the resentful wife of some Collector of Taxes, on the arm of a gentleman Duncan Gregg's senior.

And Gregg himself? Paul Martiny smiled. He'd be there all right but only just, squiring the wife of some Hooghly Pilot. Aunt Lilian had had excellent manners but she must have burst herself suppressing a giggle. In later years when he'd made a great fortune Duncan Gregg had gone up the ladder a little. But not very much, he was still in trade. A Commissioner of Municipal Sewage was a very much more important man, though Gregg's firm, of which he was now the head, made the money which paid this worthy's salary.

And now she was very old indeed, mewed up in an expensive Home, held alone at another woman's pleasure, and Paul Martiny strongly suspected she was the object of very unscrupulous pressures. He wasn't going to tolerate that; he was prepared to be very tough indeed if Dorothy Tellier gave more trouble.

In the event he had no need to be for Mrs Tellier knew when she'd stepped near the limit. She said nothing this morning of doctors or sickness: instead she opened the door with aplomb.

'Lady Gregg is rather better this morning.'

'I'm delighted the doctor thinks so too.' Paul was perfectly sure there had been no doctor.

'My daughter will take you along.'

Charlotte did so; she led them to Lilian Gregg's bedsitter which looked out on the tidy, hideous garden. She was sitting in a straight-backed chair, as upright as ever, her hands on her knees. The hands were now claws but still beautifully kept. Charlotte had left them quite alone.

Paul Martiny kissed the old lady gently. Miraculously she was never incontinent and her breath was still sweet as a garden in spring. The gesture had seemed to take her aback but she did not turn her head to refuse it.

'I'm afraid you still won't persuade me, gentlemen.'

'I'm sorry if I'm seeming stupid. Persuade you of what?'

'That it's all in the Bible.' She chuckled ironically. The sound was alarming but wholly appropriate. 'If I believe then I'll go to a place called heaven and if I don't I'll go somewhere much hotter than India.'

... So she thinks we're some form of dotty evangelist. Mrs Tellier tried to turn us away but she lets in any old crazy biblebasher. I doubt if they got much change from this one but of course they could chalk it up as a call.

'We're not men of religion, you know, aunt Lilian. In point of fact I'm Paul Martiny and this is another relation, Mike Horan.'

'Ah yes,' she said, 'how stupid I am.' Her manners

were as good as ever but it seemed she had no idea who they were.

Not one of her good days, Paul privately thought, but he checked the reflection—he wasn't quite sure. It was true that she had been talking nonsense, she hadn't flickered an eyelid when he'd given their names, but there was something behind the clear blue eyes which was a long way short of real senility. Perhaps it paid her in this curious life to pretend to be further gone than she was. That would be cunning and Paul regretted it. It always shocked him when he saw intelligence debased to the tricks of a helpless old age. Aunt Lilian might be putting it on a bit. He couldn't be sure and was left at a loss. Horan rescued him by speaking himself.

'I'm glad to see you looking so well.'

'I'm too damned well,' she said surprisingly. 'There's only one place for me now—in wood.'

Paul was sure of it now, she'd been acting from habit. He tested her. 'That's a long way away.'

'Don't be foolish. I've nothing to fear from death.'

Mrs Tellier had come in to join them, her hands clasped before her, her manner professional. Paul looked at Lilian Gregg again. She had put out the spark, she was back in her part. She said weakly to Mrs Dorothy Tellier, forcing herself to enunciate clearly: 'I've greatly enjoyed these gentlemen's visit.'

'But we mustn't let them tire you out.'

Paul rose but didn't move to go. He had caught a faint movement of Lilian's hands. It wasn't strong enough to signal to Tellier, who, whatever else she was, wasn't sensitive, but it stopped Paul Martiny dead in his tracks. Aunt Lilian still had something to say and this blundering woman had stopped her saying it. He went over to her and took her hand, bending his head politely, near hers. In his ear she said in the clearest whisper:

'My diamonds. I want Michael to have them.'

'It was kind of you to see us,' he told her. What he heard was a very unsenile; 'Good boy.'

Mrs Tellier unctuously showed them out. 'It's sad to see her like that,' she said.

'Oh yes, it's very sad indeed. Of course we shall be coming again.'

'If her doctor—' Mrs Tellier began.

'We've had that one,' Paul Martiny said brutally.

'I do not understand you, sir.' Mrs Tellier was a very offended woman.

'I believe you understand me perfectly.'

They went to the car and drove back to *The Bull*. There Paul asked crisply: 'What did you make of that?'

'Very little. But it wasn't as I'd expected it.'

'No?'

'There was something I couldn't quite put in its place.'

'Nor I at first but I'd bet on it now. Aunt Lilian finds life very much easier if she pretends to be completely senile. But she isn't quite that, or she wasn't this morning.'

'You think so?'

'I'm perfectly sure of it now. You saw me bend down to say goodbye? She gave me a message.' Paul passed it succinctly.

'Diamonds,' Mike said. 'I've never heard tell of them.'

'Nor have I, but I mean to find out at once. Can you camp here for a day or two?'

'Certainly.'

'Then ring me in London if anything happens.'

When the two men had gone the two women quarrelled, or came as close to it as either dared. The restraint on the daughter was fear of her mother, since if Dorothy became really vicious, something she would do if crossed, she could renege on their plan and leave Charlotte standing, holding the baby or rather Melsome, a man she didn't even like and who wouldn't have more than a parson's stipend. Dorothy in turn trod carefully. Respectability was her private god, and her daughter, if she did her an injury, could blow that out of the window conclusively. Her affair with Heale-Mann hadn't troubled her conscience. It had been conducted with a most searching discretion and had been good for Mrs Tellier's health, but the last thing she wanted, though perhaps she'd survive it, was public knowledge of it in a place like Westercombe where she made more than a modestly adequate living by running a Home for rich old ladies. And Charlotte could be nasty too, her father had been a nasty man.

She was saying and sounding unhappy to say it: 'It's very awkward about that doctor dying. It leaves only one man to support the new Will.'

'One should be enough, I think.'

'You're not thinking, Mother, you're simply hoping.'

Mrs Tellier let pass with an effort. 'It's too late to do anything now.'

'I know. But if anything happened to Gilbert Heale-Mann that Will would be just a piece of paper. Someone challenges it, and you know who I mean, and very likely we wouldn't win the case.'

'Why should anything happen to Gilbert, please? He's a perfectly healthy man, still virile.' He was, she was thinking, provided you helped him. You helped him every fortnight, not more. She hadn't heard he had died that morning.

'I didn't say anything would but it might. In which case we'd be wide, wide open.'

'What do you know of Michael Horan? I gather he lives in the same house as you do.'

'We say "Good morning" in the hall—that's all.' She'd once given him an evident opening but he hadn't even invited her in. That was to be regretted now. He had seemed to be well enough off for a present and a knowledge of his character, the sort you only obtained in bed, would be an asset which she'd have welcomed warmly. Alas she didn't have that asset but she did have another, a knowledge of Paul. She hesitated to tell her mother but they were in this together or not at all; she said finally, choosing her words with care:

'Horan alone might not be dangerous, but he comes here with Paul Martiny—that's ominous. You told me they'd never done that before, and Paul never told me he'd even met Horan.'

'At one time I gather you knew him quite well.' Dorothy Tellier knew perfectly well that the question was something less than tactful, but she disapproved of her daughter's way of life and the temptation to wound another woman was one which she could never resist.... 'At one time'—that would certainly sting.

It stung brutally but Charlotte rode it; she said with what she hoped was dignity:

'At one time we were living together.' She was privately thinking that put it too high, but it sounded better, very much better, than saying: 'We spent a week in Venice.' Just the same a week had been more than enough. You could learn all you needed of most men alive from a mutually agreeable week.

'Who you sleep with—'

'Whom.'

'—is no business of mine.'

'I agree with that, Mother, I really do.'

'But in this case it may have done some good. You say you know nothing of Michael Horan but you must know something about this Martiny.'

'Oh yes,' Charlotte said, 'I do indeed.'

'You don't want to tell me?'

'I don't but I must. I think he's a charming but dangerous man.'

'I don't think he's charming, he's terribly rude. He practically called me a liar.'

'Now did he?'

For an instant they both looked over the edge onto something which would be really serious. Then Charlotte drew back; she needed her mother. 'We were talking about Paul Martiny. I think that manner of his is very deceptive.'

'And how does that affect us—both of us?'

'He's a man with a pretty strong sense of family. I don't mean he's any sort of snob—rather the reverse, I think—but if he thought there was any sort of swindle he'd fight like a wild cat for what he thought proper.'

Dorothy let the 'swindle' go by. 'You mean he'd back Horan?'

'Yes I do.'

'But Clement's a relation too.'

'That wouldn't matter—not to Paul. He wouldn't care much who got the money provided it was the old lady's wishes. But if he thought that one of his precious family, I mean the old bag you keep upstairs, had been influenced into changing her mind . . .'

Charlotte left it unfinished and both were silent. For the first time Dorothy Tellier was frightened, for her private impression of Paul Martiny had not been so different from Charlotte's own. And her guess was that his nose had been working, he had picked up some scent and would follow it up. In which case he could be more than dangerous. Whosoever the witnesses, Wills could be challenged. Martiny might back Horan in doing so and it was evident that he didn't lack money. He could make any lawsuit disastrously expensive.

Men, Dorothy thought—impossible men. Especially men with a family conscience.

Her daughter's thoughts were also of conscience, though they ran on very different lines. She didn't dare tell her mother her worry, which was simply that Clement would ruin it all. That conscience of his was tiresome—contemptible. Even if the Will stood up, even if they laid hands on the money, he was capable of extreme stupidity. The fool had even talked of it: the poorer members of his wretched family must of course be looked after properly first, and then he had nattered on about charities, charities in India too. India! You could have it for nothing.

But she shrugged for she wasn't by any means hopeless. Once married to Clement she believed she could manage him. She knew much about men. Oh yes, she could handle him.

She had thought this before and she thought it again. For the second time she was gravely mistaken.

11

Charlotte Tellier had been mistaken in principle, a matter which would not have distressed her, but she had also been gravely mistaken in timing. For Clement hadn't waited for marriage before cleansing his conscience of nagging doubt. He was wet but he wasn't crassly stupid, and even in a country parish, where one learnt little of the wider world, he'd had several and sad occasions to see what marriage could do to the weaker partner. He hadn't a doubt which that would be. In his own strange way he wanted Charlotte; she represented a sort of salvation which he had tried before to find and failed. Very well, she would probably boss him to death but she wouldn't boss his Christian conscience.

So he had motored back to Westercombe and gone to *The Bull* to talk to Horan. It hadn't been convenient since he'd had to return to his parish for Sunday; the distance was considerable and his car was both ageing and far from fast. Nevertheless when his mind was made up he had gone to some trouble to carry his plan out. He had looked up Horan's number in London, and when the telephone had stayed unanswered he'd assumed, since he had met him there, that Horan must have stayed on in Westercombe. Three more telephone calls, the first two unfruitful, but the third tracked Horan down at *The Bull*. Melsome could ill afford this expense but had faced it since he believed he must. In an affair of what he saw as a duty expense was a matter which had to come second. He had no idea that Michael Horan was the man who had stood to inherit before him, for the Telliers had adroitly stalled on the one occasion (he hadn't dared more) when he'd raised a vague query about Lilian's intentions before she had made a Will in his favour.

The stall had surprised him but not raised his suspicions, for in his pastoral life he'd seen similar cases. Rich old parties who'd lived amoral lives—he couldn't bring himself to the straight condemnation of calling an aunt a wicked old woman—rich old parties when they felt Death's breath would sometimes try to compound their sins by buying their way through the gates of heaven. Sometimes they set up Trusts for charity, sometimes they gave to organizations whose officials, if rumour were worth belief, lived lives which were something more than comfortable. It was in this tradition to leave to a clergyman, a man who would have a sense of trust. As indeed Clement had, they had drummed it into him. All property was a trust before God, one the holder would be called to account for when he came before his Maker for judgement.

So Melsome had not been too much astonished, but later, in the quiet of his Rectory, doubts had crept in to cloud the first vision. He was far from being a worldly man but certain facts were there, inescapable, and it wouldn't be right to shut his eyes to them. The first was that he was marrying Charlotte; the second old Lady Gregg's, well, shakiness; the third that his future mother-in-law held this failing old lady in a Home called *The Laurels*.

Clement Melsome had prayed for guidance. It came. It was none of his business to probe more deeply, indeed he couldn't even put feelers out without bitterly offending the Telliers and that would be no start to his marriage, but more than ever he must invoke his principles. Legally he was no Trustee, all this money was being bequeathed absolutely, but he held it in trust just the same. So live up to it. He had drifted away from his other kinsmen, but Horan he'd met a few days ago so Horan was the man to start on. It wouldn't be easy, it was going to need tact, but like most Anglican clergymen he believed he had bags of it.

He called on Horan in the afternoon, finding him asleep in bed. Clement Melsome hid a mild disapproval. Afternoon sleeping was vaguely pagan and therefore to be vaguely deprecated. Michael for his part was very annoyed. He was a man who slept extremely well and enjoyed the physical act of sleeping. On top of that it struck him as cool—cool on Melsome's part and cool on *The Bull's*. The afternoon was a private time, whether for golf or reading or sleeping: one gentleman didn't disturb another; and as for *The Bull* it was all somewhat casual. *The Bull* didn't advertise phones in bedrooms, but to send up a caller with no more than the boot boy was something below a seemly standard.

But the boot boy knocked twice and Mike Horan woke. Clement Melsome came in and bowed with formality. Mike Horan sat up in bed in pyjamas. He was ruffled in more than one sense and looked it.

'My name's Clement Melsome. We met at *The Laurels*.'

'Of course. Please sit down.' Horan waved at the single and tatty armchair.

'Also we're some sort of distant relations.'

'I'm in no position to contradict you.'

The answer threw Melsome severely off stride. A second reason he'd come to Horan first was that he'd heard that he had done time in prison. He was therefore an outstanding candidate for the helping hand which money could offer. And here was this jailbird blocking advances. Clement Melsome was not at ease and showed it. Inevitably he began to wuffle, his manner a mixture of unction and nervousness.

'You must forgive me if I've disturbed your rest. I've come to offer you reassurance.'

'Whatever about?' Mike Horan asked. He hadn't much liked the look of Melsome. He had noticed the Roman-style clerical collar, the flabby hands, the incipient belly.

It was a reasonable question but harshly delivered, and Melsome hadn't expected the harshness. He began to wuffle more than ever.

'We're relations, you know.'

'So you said. Very distant ones.'

'But I feel that I owe you a duty.'

'Indeed?'

Melsome drew a long breath and prayed again. 'In the event,' he said, 'that I meet good fortune I shall not be unmindful of family kinship.'

'Please put it in English.'

He tried again. 'It's money,' he said.

'You're in trouble with money?'

'No, no. The reverse. I am about to inherit some, quite a lot I believe.'

'My heartiest congratulations.'

'You must realize that as a priest I have principles.'

Horan was moving quite close to anger. At first he had been no more than irritated, he hated to be woken from sleep, but the pomposity, the circumlocution, were hard to take and hard increasingly; he said acidly:

'You greatly surprise me. I thought the Church of England boasted that it was all things to all men and damn the doctrine.'

Clement Melsome didn't like this a bit, as an Anglo-Catholic he deeply resented it, but he hadn't come here to make a convert. 'I fear you elect to misunderstand me. I meant personal principles.'

'Stuff about money?'

'Yes, that is so.' Under any sort of embarrassment Clement Melsome became more pompous than ever. 'You may rely upon me to do my duty. My duty to the whole of the family.'

Mike Horan clenched his fingers hard, but if he hit this dim priest he would probably maim him. 'You mentioned money?'

Melsome nodded.

'You mentioned your principles?'

'Yes indeed.'

'You also spoke of the family?'

'Quite.'

'Are you offering me money, please?' The voice had gone up a dangerous half tone but Melsome didn't notice the change.

'When I'm able to do justice I shall.'

'I'm afraid I think you're a clumsy fool.'

Mike Horan had got out of bed, moving to the door and opening it. Melsome went out without assault but the effort cost more than he'd ever know.

Mike Horan went back to his bed and lay down on it. He began to laugh, quite close to hysteria. The insolence of it, the shattering patronage! From *The Laurels* the stink of corruption rose fetidly, and he'd already agreed with Martiny's guess that the festering flesh was some form of Will-fiddle. But now he knew something Martiny didn't; he knew beyond a reasonable doubt what form the fiddle had taken and why. Mrs Tellier's daughter was marrying Melsome so they'd got at an almost helpless old lady, used pressures which he could easily guess, made her change her Will in Melsome's favour. And Melsome with his pathetic principles had blown the whole conspiracy open.

His anger faded to a different emotion and Mike Horan knew its name. It was fear. It was fear of himself, of the way his bile worked. Three things would stir it and Michael knew them. The first was simply patronage. He'd just had that and had somehow controlled himself, but the second was a more powerful stimulus—being taken for a bloody fool. The third and most potent goad of all was being leant on for that scorched his pride.

He tried to relax but found it difficult; he knew himself, he was unpredictable. And it was one shot gone and two to go. Mike Horan was fearful that someone would fire them since he knew what was going to happen then. He'd lose his temper again and do something fatal.

When he was calmer he rang up Martiny, telling him what had happened shortly.

'That's interesting—that clears the air. We were both of us guessing before. Now we know. There's another Will and this parson's the heir.'

' "Who will rid me of this insolent priest?" '

'It was an impertinence,' Paul Martiny conceded. 'Well-intentioned perhaps, but still an impertinence.' He added on a note of anxiety, 'What did you do?'

'I didn't do anything.'

'I'm delighted to hear it. Country parsons, even wickedly wet ones, are an article in short supply.'

Michael Horan laughed. 'And there's something else quite apart from that priest. I heard them talking about it down in the bar. There's been another accident here.'

'Westercombe sounds a dangerous place.'

'I'm serious, though. It was one to a lawyer.'

'What lawyer?'

'The solicitor here. A man called Heale-Mann.'

'He practised in Westercombe?'

'Very successfully.'

There was a full minute's silence till Martiny spoke again. 'A doctor and a solicitor. Normal witnesses to any Will, classic witnesses to anything fishy. Is he dead?'

'Very dead.'

'Coincidence,' Paul Martiny said, 'is something one must sometimes accept. But we certainly cannot afford to accept it when we're on the wrong end of a Tellier swindle.'

'What are we going to do?'

'I've got to find out about those diamonds. Whether the baubles really exist, and if they do where the old lady kept them.'

'But you're coming back here?'

'Of course I am, but I've an inquiry to make in

London first. If I'm right in a guess we may hold four aces. The Telliers can keep any Will they've cooked up and the Telliers can use it rudely.'

Paul Martiny had told Michael Horan that he had an inquiry to make in London. He made it. When Lilian Gregg had whispered of diamonds she had done so without a hint of senility, but since she hadn't told him where they were (perhaps with Dorothy Tellier present she'd been frightened of even a further whisper) it was Paul Martiny's business to find them. He could of course make formal inquiries, but the Telliers would soon find out he had done so, and it was no part of Paul Martiny's plan that the Telliers should lay hands on these diamonds.

That is, if they in fact existed, and he wasn't entirely sure of that. He was convinced the old lady often shammed, parading an increasing senescence at moments when her mind was lucid, but it was also true she was very old and the old were often confused and imagined things. . . . Diamonds—what diamonds? On the face of it it sounded improbable: diamonds weren't the late Sir Duncan's form. It wasn't that he was ever ungenerous to a wife who, though she had horned him shamelessly, he'd respected and valued right up to the end. But diamonds earned no income whatever and Sir Duncan had been a businessman. There was only one way to find out and Paul took it. He called on Lilian Gregg's London bankers.

They were also his own and the connection a close one. Paul caused money which he knew was stolen to reappear in other countries, but whether his cousin Kenneth Leigh suspected this fact he did not know.

Cousin Kenneth who was Chairman of Edlers would have regarded that as Martiny's business; to the best of his knowledge these sums were clean, and if Paul was choosing to break the law the respectable House of Edlers was not.

It wasn't breaking the law but it was bending it double and doing so with a happy gusto. Kenneth Leigh had no time for legislation which sought to obstruct the free flow of money. His dislike of it wasn't academic, some theory learnt in three years at Cambridge that capital had an inalienable right to seek profits in the most profitable field; it was intenser than that and far more personal. In a bankrupt and degenerate country, sick with envy disguised as social justice, any man with a little money to spare was a fool if he didn't get it out.

Kenneth Leigh had often done this for Paul and had assumed that he wanted the same again. But Paul, as he sat down, said:

'Aunt Lilian.'

'I haven't seen her for years.'

'I saw her this week. She's pretty dicky but she isn't quite senile. She mentioned her diamonds.'

Cousin Kenneth repeated Mike Horan's words. 'I've never heard tell of any diamonds.'

'You don't hold them here?'

'Indeed we do not.'

The banker was silent, thinking hard. He owed a duty to Lilian Gregg, his customer, a duty of complete discretion, but Paul was a man of his own close-knit world and moreover, like Martiny himself, he had a strong sense of family obligation. Aunt Lilian Gregg was very old and living in a Home for the Elderly.

Some of them were perfectly scrupulous but the banker had also heard stories of others. So Martiny whom he wholly trusted had come to him about Lilian Gregg. Very well, he would help if he could and dared. But he left Paul Martiny to make the running.

'Assuming they exist,' Paul said, 'would you care to guess where they are if not here?'

'Another bank?'

'She wouldn't have had one.'

'A safe deposit, then?'

'Not her form.'

'Her solicitors, do you think?'

'I do not.'

'You seem very sure but I won't ask you why.' To the banker this beautifully formal game had reached a point where he felt he could lead himself. 'Let me tell you something,' he said, 'in confidence. You're assuming aunt Lilian Gregg is rich?'

'She ought to be very cosy indeed. Sir Duncan made a handsome pile, and even when milked by outrageous Duty she should still be what I myself would call rich.'

'Her account at this bank is five thousand pounds.'

'If I didn't know you as well as I do I should say that I found it hard to believe you.'

Kenneth Leigh rang for sherry and smiled urbanely. 'Speaking as a banker *pur sang* I've already stepped over the line of propriety. Since I've done so I'm going to tell you some more.' He poured the sherry and sipped it happily. 'You remember that awful house of theirs?'

'Yes.'

'I take it you've been there?'

'Several times.'

'Then you know what sort of house it was—nine bedrooms or so and two acres of parkland. Anywhere in the commuter belt and the thing would have been worth a fortune, or rather the two acres would. But three miles out of Westercombe it wasn't worth anything like a fortune. The house was much too big to live in but also too small for an institution, and the park was sold off to a neighbouring farmer. So they're knocking it down now for what it contains, and as you've seen it you'll know that that's hardly classic. Aunt Lilian used some of the proceeds to buy that villa she later lived in in Westercombe, where she pigged it with that appalling companion till she threw her out and moved off to *The Laurels*. There's been difficulty about that villa too. The Council bought it to turn into flats but they changed their minds and haven't done so. At the moment it's boarded up, going to pot. Aunt Lilian got paid for it, though.' The banker drank a little more sherry. 'You are wondering why I'm reciting all this when you've probably heard most before?'

'You usually have good reason, cousin.'

'In this case it's arithmetic. Listen. What she got from that thing which they called a manor, plus later the price of the Westercombe villa, aunt Lilian paid into us and left it. She told us to pay her bills till she died. We have done so and there's five thousand left. I hope with luck it will see her out because she doesn't possess another penny.'

'I'd like something a little stronger than sherry, please.'

'Whisky?'

'Not before luncheon.'

'Then gin?'

'A very large gin with ice and lemon.'

The gin was brought and Martiny drank it. 'I'm going to be indiscreet,' he said.

'I hope not since I'd like to help you. Take it easy, crawl round it, and maybe I can.'

'Her portfolio, then?'

'I can't give you details.' It was regretful but also firm.

Paul Martiny didn't press the point: the securities had obviously gone. 'Could you tell me where they went?'

'At a stretch. A month before she moved to *The Laurels* she sold them through uncle Laurence, our broker. The sum involved was pretty big and she paid it into her current account.'

'Which stands at five thousand pounds?'

'That is so.'

Paul Martiny rose to take his leave but his cousin waved him firmly down. He was a banker with all a banker's instincts but this was family business; he trusted Paul.... Old aunt Lilian—he had always liked her. If somebody was trying to swindle her and that was what he'd begun to suspect—if somebody was trying to take her he wouldn't stand smugly aside and let them. Rules, he remembered, were made for fools, and Paul Martiny was far from that.

'I'm going to tell you something else, and I won't insult you by talking of confidence. That money stood in the old lady's account for a matter of three days —no more. Then she drew out an almost equal sum.'

'In cash?'

'Not in cash.'

For the first time the banker showed hesitation. He knew that this was the final fence and it was one which all his training shied at. But he'd come so far and he meant to finish. Paul helped him out of an indecision.

'She drew it all out on a single cheque?'

'Yes, cousin Paul, she did just that.'

This time Kenneth Leigh didn't stop him as he rose and began to move to the door. 'I'm very grateful indeed,' Paul Martiny said.

'A pleasure to help as it always is.'

Leigh swung the fine panelled door wide open and as Paul went past him said very softly:

'That cheque was made out to a famous jeweller.'

12

Paul went back to his room to make his plan, now certain that the diamonds existed, though why his aunt had bought them he couldn't guess. Perhaps she had always wanted diamonds as some women carried a yen to their graves, or perhaps she had borrowed her husband's shrewdness and had seen a wicked inflation coming. So she'd put aside enough to live on and Gregg capital was protected in stones. But her motive was of little importance: what mattered was the task she had left him.

They wouldn't be in the big house, now a shell; and when she had moved to Westercombe she'd still owned a very substantial portfolio. Cousin Kenneth had made it clear she had sold it, but that had been while she'd lived at the small one. Three days after selling she had drawn out the proceeds and paid them to an eminent jeweller. So the old house had never held those diamonds.

But that house could be something more than important, for as he'd told Cousin Kenneth Paul Martiny had been in it, and once she had shown him her secret hidey-hole, a sliding panel in the Edwardian mantel. He had hidden a smile as she proudly did so for it had struck him as indifferent security. Probably all the servants knew of it, but a rogue would not have been greatly tempted by what the hidey-hole held—some trinkets and a cash float for the house-keeping.

Yet the elderly were creatures of habit. She might have put a similar hidey-hole somewhere in the Westercombe villa. Might. It was quite a big might on any count, but if she had it was at least explicable if she had left her prize there when she moved to *The Laurels*. One explanation would be simply forgetfulness, since there were days when her mind was in fact as feeble as on the others when she pretended senility; and another would be conscious cunning. What had she said? 'I want Michael to have them.' Five thousand pounds in the bank—no Duty. But diamonds worth several hundred thousand were something you'd wish to pass directly, understandable if you were very old, born in another age and climate, more than that if you lived to today. Only sensible.

It was worth a try—very well worth it. If it didn't come off he'd have to ask her, but that would mean official inquiries. When he couldn't conceal the stones' existence. And Paul Martiny had a stronger motive than the wish to avoid a crippling Duty. There was Will-trouble now—he was perfectly sure of it. So if he found these diamonds he'd give them to Mike, that was what aunt Lilian wanted, and the Telliers could keep their new Will and the estate of three thousand pounds which it covered. Rather neat, Paul considered, a very real justice. Not the justice of the Courts which he loathed, but a natural justice, and therefore satisfying.

And what had Leigh said about the villa? There'd been trouble and it was going to pot. Probably it had been vandalized, so the Council would board it up and wire it. Paul had seen a dozen similar and it wouldn't be hard to effect an entry. He slipped round a corner and bought what he needed, a hammer, stout chisel, wirecutters, torch. Then he fetched his car and drove to Westercombe. He found a room vacant but not at *The Bull*, for Mike Horan was still at *The Bull* awaiting him and Paul didn't fancy an abstract discussion. He preferred to lay down something concrete.

Which he dared to hope would be Lilian's diamonds.

He went to bed early and set his alarm, and at two o'clock in the morning crept out. Westercombe was entirely deserted. The street lights were out except in the square but there was the last of a moon and he'd taken his torch. He had been to the villa so knew where it was, and as he walked towards it, away from the square, there wasn't a movement and almost no sound. Once a dog barked and that was all. A roaming cat slunk past him silently. In the middle distance the sea sighed softly. It had the eeriness of small towns in the small hours.

Paul found the villa and reconnoitred it carefully. It was much as he had supposed it would be, the garden a shambles, the windows boarded. Most of them were also wired but on one of them the wire had been cut. He put the chisel behind the boarding and levered, astonished when it came cleanly away. He caught it before it fell and used his torch. The nail holes were there but not the nails. The panel had been standing free.

... Somebody's camping here inside.

Paul Martiny stood still and thought. This was a complication—most awkward. With a couple of tramps sleeping rough inside he could hardly make a proper search, and if he did and they woke he'd be risking a beating. Nevertheless he'd come so far ...

He put a leg across the broken windowsill. As he'd thought the window was smashed to pieces. Glass littered the floor of the room. It was empty. Paul pulled the other leg after him cautiously.

The first sense to signal was that of smell, the unmistakable stink of human excrement.

... They're living very rough indeed but at least they've chosen to do it upstairs.

Paul knew that this room had once been the study and the hopes he'd had had been centred on it. Picking his way through the splintered glass he moved to the mantel and went over it thoroughly. It took him all of twenty minutes and at the end he was sure that there wasn't a slide.

Paul stood still again, this time hesitating. The next best bet was aunt Lilian's bedroom but that was upstairs and he wasn't a hero. He could earn himself something worse than a beating.

So he hesitated but he finally moved, feeling his way up the broken stairs. The smell was getting steadily worse and Paul Martiny suppressed a retch. He came to the landing, the bedroom doors. One was ajar and he pushed it open.

The stench was overpowering now and in the light of the torch Paul Martiny saw why. There were also two piles of filthy blankets and on them two human figures, sleeping. They seemed to be sleeping very hard, for the door, when Paul moved it, had creaked a warning. He shone his torch on the first body—a girl. She'd been pretty once but was now a wreck. Saliva slid out of her mouth obscenely. The other was apparently male, though his hair was as long as the girl's and dirtier.

He woke in the light of the torch and groaned, then he pulled himself upright clumsily. The action seemed to have cost him an effort. He blinked and said thickly:

'Who are you?'

The girl hadn't moved and Paul had guessed why. These weren't drunks, they were hopheads, high as kites.

Paul didn't answer. There wasn't a good one.

'Get lost,' the man said, 'and leave us alone.'

'What you need is a doctor. I'll send one round.'

They were the first words which came to Paul's shaken mind, a natural and human reaction; he didn't know at the time they were also the worst. They appeared to enrage the man insanely. He pulled himself to his feet and glowered.

'Mind your own bloody business. Get out of here.'

Paul's silence pushed the man over his edge. He snarled and produced a knife. He waved it. Paul retreated two paces. It was lucky he did so.

The man spoke again, but Paul didn't catch it. He was watching the knife, decidedly frightened. He knew nothing of brawling in any form, and though this man was drugged and shaky he could get in a strike and do serious damage. Paul Martiny could bleed to death in a sewer.

In the event the man did no damage whatever. He made his rush but his legs betrayed him. The two paces Paul had retreated saved him. The man stumbled and fell; the knife fell too. As he went down he banged his head. He did not move again. The girl snored.

Paul didn't bother to pick up the knife but went

124

to the mantel and felt the moulding. A panel shifted first time and Paul looked in. In the light of his torch the stones glittered brilliantly.

He pulled them out and whistled softly. He was a man who managed criminals' business and occasionally he would handle stones, though only when he knew a safe market. He had more than an amateur's knowledge of diamonds and these were very good indeed. Not a necklace which, however well-matched, would be hard to disguise by cutting again, but a pendant with five tremendous stones each of them worth a solid fortune. Paul knew where he could deal for cash—Mike Horan would have no use for diamonds.

He put the pendant in an inside pocket, shutting the slide of the hidey-hole carefully. The man and the girl hadn't moved an inch.

Drop-outs, Paul thought, and faeces all over. Diamonds within five feet of their heads. Something around three hundred thousand, though he wouldn't be getting the whole of that.

He drove back to London, sent a postcard to Horan. He'd be going to Amsterdam for two days and would be staying at *The Doelen* hotel.

13

Like many determined and forceful women, Dorothy Tellier, when under pressure, could come suddenly close to physical panic. At this moment she wasn't wringing her hands but they were gripped upon her still handsome thighs in a tension which didn't escape her daughter. 'This is terrible,' she was saying, 'terrible. Both of them gone like that in a week.'

'I agree that it's extremely awkward.' Charlotte was playing it cool since she had to. The warning lights were out and flashing. Her mother had some absurd new plan.

'That man Michael Horan has murdered them both.'

'Oh come, Mother, that isn't sensible.'

'Who else had a motive?'

'I don't know that but you're jumping the gun. You're assuming that these were murders—I'm not. They could have been—it's perfectly possible—but until that's established I don't accept it.'

'You're simply being difficult.'

'No. Accident or deliberate murder the effect on us is just the same. Without that doctor and your solicitor friend that Will is just a piece of paper, or it will be if someone stands up and challenges it.'

'Then what do you mean to do?'

'I must think.'

'I,' Mrs Tellier said, 'have done so. We must make another Will.'

'Absurd.' Charlotte was fighting a rising despair.

Her mother, in this mood, might do anything.

'And why absurd?' Mrs Tellier was getting angry now but Charlotte preferred her anger to panic.

'Too suspicious to stand up for a minute. A whole series of Wills, one, two, three—I ask you.'

'Then we must get the existing one witnessed again. I happen to know another solicitor.'

'You seem to have had a thing for solicitors.' The jibe had been deliberate, an attempt to set Mrs Tellier off on a conventional row between mother and daughter. It was something which Charlotte had often handled, whereas a frightened Dorothy frightened her too. But Dorothy declined the bait firmly.

'And there's that doctor you know in London.'

'Karl?' This time Charlotte Tellier laughed. Karl had been a psychiatrist and though he made a very good living in a practice which might be described as fashionable, he didn't have British qualifications, and his guttural Middle Europe accent, the fact that he'd talk to a court in jargon, would be precisely what English judges loathed most. As any sort of expert witness Karl would guarantee that you'd lose your case.

'What's wrong with Karl?'

'I needn't tell you. What's important is that I haven't seen him for over three years and maybe more.'

'You're being difficult again.'

'I am not. I think both your plans are out of the question but I've another myself and I'm going to sleep on it.'

'You must tell me, Charlotte.'

'I would if it needed your help but it doesn't.'

Mrs Tellier snorted but finally rose. 'I don't think

my plans are absurd at all, and who are you to give legal advice? I shall go up to London by train to-morrow and there I shall see my friend.'

'You'll get nowhere.'

Mrs Tellier's plans for another Will, new witnesses for the old one, more fiddling, had not impressed a realistic daughter. She considered these plans were conceived in panic as certainly they'd been explained in a dither and she knew when a path had come to its end. She herself knew another which she believed had a chance.

She was basing her hopes on two simple factors: first that her impression of Horan was one of a man who would listen to reason, and second that she was still an attractive woman. It was true that he had once rebuffed her, mildly no doubt but he'd still declined, but her charms were the lesser of two strong weapons, the more powerful an appeal to reason, to mutual advantage, the avoidance of conflict.

Nevertheless she dressed herself carefully before walking to *The Bull* to see Horan. Not flashily—that would put him off—but to emphasize she was still a woman and a very well-endowed one at that. One should never neglect a well-tried tool though this morning it wasn't her principal armament.

She found Horan in the bar with a drink and he offered her another amiably. They took them to deep armchairs in a corner and Charlotte said coolly:

'You weren't expecting me.'

'Frankly I was not,' he said. She could see that he wouldn't be making it easy, but nor had he refused to see her. He had in fact bought her a gin and tonic. She put out another feeler quickly.

'We're not necessarily enemies.'

He didn't react to this as she'd hoped. 'I don't know why you should think we were.'

'Is that as frank as you were before?'

Michael Horan smiled. 'Perhaps not quite.'

She saw she would have to clear the air. He wasn't precisely fending her off but nor was he conceding openings, and the best way to clear the air was thoroughly. 'That Will,' she said and watched his face.

To her great relief he nodded quietly. If he'd said: 'What Will?' he'd have halted her awkwardly. Encouraged she played another card. 'You are thinking the same as I am?'

'Probably. If you're telling me there's a new Will we'd guessed it.'

She let the plural pass in silence. 'That Will could cause a great deal of trouble. Litigation. The usual lawyer's benefit.'

'Since you say so,' he said.

'And I don't like trouble.'

This time he did help her actively. 'So you've come to me with a proposition?'

'If you call it that.'

'It's a good enough word.'

She saw that the sparring was finally over. He would listen to what she wished to say though how he would take it she couldn't yet guess. 'Let's avoid any litigation.'

'How?'

'By making a private arrangement between ourselves.'

'Please state your terms.'

'You don't challenge the Will.'

'I had followed that.'

'In return we will cut you in.'

'How much?'

He wasn't greatly interested but he was curious to hear what she'd say. The Telliers were unusual people. It would be fascinating to hear what they thought would tempt a man to accept a compromise.

'Twenty thousand pounds,' she said.

His face didn't change since he didn't permit it. Twenty thousand pounds, he was thinking, out of what could hardly be less than a quarter million. Still two thousand short of his debt to Lucas. In matters of commerce the fault of the Dutch is in giving too little and asking too much. Did the Telliers have Dutch blood? It seemed possible.

'Eighty per cent of the net estate.'

She realized at once she had lost him fatally. A demand for anything up to fifty could be taken as negotiation, and she was ready to settle for forty happily, but eighty was the clearest sign-off. He simply wasn't interested in a split of the loot to save himself trouble. Well, she still had another weapon. She used it. She leant expertly out of her chair towards him. She was good at it for she'd done it often, and often it had worked very well.

His expression should have warned her but didn't. He wasn't bent, he liked good red meat, but he liked it as he ordered it, not brashly slapped down on a plate in front of him. Since he didn't speak she was forced to lead again.

'We could deal with the money on more personal terms.'

'I thought you intended to marry Melsome.'

'Clement,' she said. 'I think you've met him.'

Again he didn't rise to it and again she had to throw a fly. 'There are other things in life than money.'

'But few of them that money won't buy. The exceptions are not for sale in any case.'

'Don't you ever gamble, Michael?'

He ignored that she'd used his Christian name. 'I gamble very seldom indeed and when I do I get into trouble.'

... Twenty-two thousand pounds and a beating, still a debt to that wholly loathsome Lucas. There were two things she couldn't tempt him with: one was her body, the other a gamble. But if she hadn't been insultingly greedy he might possibly have heard her out, conceivably thought a real offer over. But no, she had started at twenty thousand.

She takes me for a perfect fool.

He rose and she rose reluctantly with him, and they walked to the door of the cosy bar. At it she reverted disastrously: her mother came unmistakably uppermost.

'You'll regret this,' she said.

'Only time will tell.'

He went back to the bar and another drink; he was angry but less than he'd once expected.... How had he listed the things which got to him? Patronage first and Melsome had oozed it, then the insult of underestimation, being taken for a bloody fool. Charlotte Tellier had done that and handsomely. He ought to be blindly furious but curiously he was almost indifferent, for a sense of the inevitable had watered the fires of his wicked temper. Patronage and insult—so far. That was two straight across the plate and he'd missed them. The third was going to put him out. Being leant on—that was the third pitch. Fatal. He was going to do something foolish again, but there wasn't very much point in worrying till the sardonic gods sent the third one over. Mike Horan didn't doubt they would. They had marked him and he couldn't escape it.

Mrs Tellier never went up to London for Lilian Gregg won the final victory. She woke in the small hours hearing Death's wings and prepared to go with him. She put her hands behind her head which was how she had always slept as a child, composed and reflective, unfrightened and happy.

A good life, she decided, in all senses but one and that one wasn't the least important. She hadn't been a faithful wife but nor had she cheated a man she had married. When he'd wanted her she'd been coolly available—no dressing-rooms for Sir Duncan Gregg. There were women who wouldn't approve of that but they weren't the sort she had any time for. So he'd *used* her? Those were foolish words. She'd kept him healthy and active well into his eighties, and though he must have known how she lived he had never protested or threatened a crisis. Why should he protest? He was earthy and sensible, and though she had horned him more than generously she'd never done so to his public shame.... In country houses when she'd left him in India, in hill stations with army captains, in the staterooms of the P. and O. Once in a train with a maharajah. There hadn't been a corridor and at a stop she'd gone down for a meal in the dining-car. He'd been a gorgeous, still semi-barbaric figure and his private coach had been next to the dining-car. When the train stopped again he'd suggested a brandy.

And if you had to think in words like 'using', what had she done to Duncan? Used him. She'd loved him when she'd married him but when the ecstasies had gently faded they'd been replaced by a mutual and warm respect. He'd gone back to his driving interest, money. She had never been ashamed to use it.

Of which he had made a very large sum and in a fashion which was now ill thought of. Exploitation —another emotive word. Poor Indians slaving in Hooghly mills, slightly cleaner ones picking tea in the hills, all paying toll to men like Duncan. Her laugh was as clear as a bell, a child's. She'd thought like that once, she remembered. Ridiculous. Not that she'd been alone in her error. Plenty of perfectly normal young people went to India with a sense of pity and in a year or two it had gone with the wind. Sometimes it was replaced by indifference, more often by a secret contempt. Exploited? But of course they were, and if the British hadn't got there first somebody else would have ground them harder. An educated Indian with a wholly uncharacteristic frankness had once explained to her what they felt themselves. They didn't hate us that we'd come with a sword, far less that we took what was there for the taking, but they hated us for our small efficiencies, for the facts that the trains sometimes ran to time and that an English clerk could drive in a nail straight. These were the real humiliations.

Lilian Gregg lay in total peace or almost, only a

single shadow dimming it. My diamonds, she thought
—I hope Paul finds them. Too late to see him again
and tell him, but he was the cleverest of her side of
the family and she'd noticed that he had taken her
seriously. She knew that that didn't always happen
for her bad days were very real indeed. That Will,
for instance—she remembered she'd made one but she
didn't remember what it had said. She had signed
because they had ceaselessly pestered her, that lawyer
and that stupid doctor, above all that horrible woman
Tellier. All she'd wanted was to escape them in sleep.

As she turned her face to the papered wall she
thought again of her husband Duncan. In moments
of any real emotion he had still used his native doric
pungently and a phrase of it now returned to his
wife. She said as Death gently touched her shoulder :
'My God, I've left a bugger's muddle.'

Enzo had read Rex Lucas a lecture on the difference
between the artistic killing and the journeyman affair
of mere murder. He had explained that the artistic
killing must leave at least an active doubt that it
wasn't in fact a killing at all. This had been amply
true of the doctor but rather less so of Mr Gilbert
Heale-Mann. When that Paddy collected his wits
again he'd be telling a somewhat unusual story,
though Enzo doubted that he'd ever realize that the
effects of a gross excess of alcohol had been com-
pounded by a judicious drug. But he could tell of
sharing his cups with a foreigner and he would probably deny categorically that he'd had any idea of not
working next day.

He could also describe the foreigner, but not well.

For one thing he'd been far too drunk for anything near a good description, and for another Enzo had taken some care that any description this Paddy might give would be misleading at the very lowest. He had a pro's contempt for all formal disguises—no dark glasses, no wigs or beards, no limps—but he took sensible and effective precautions. He had a very fine head of light grey hair and this he had dyed a raven black before leaving for his work in Westercombe. He had now removed the dye with care for he was properly proud of his splendid head, and the Mexican moustache, which he'd hated, had been shaved away with a grunt of relief. All this was simple but it was also effective. What the Paddy would tell a suspicious police would be near useless as identification. As for Enzo's foreign accent the next question would be 'Which foreign accent?' A drunken Irishman would hardly know, and in any case, in this year of grace, there were almost as many foreign accents walking the streets of British cities as there were people who spoke the native tongues.

So Enzo was by no means in hiding; he was staying quietly at a quiet hotel which was owned by a compatriot. Who had probably formed an opinion of Enzo but could hardly have guessed at his very real eminence and if he had would of course pretend that he hadn't.

And from this quiet hotel Enzo rang Lucas. 'I have done as you wished,' he said.

'That's good.'

'When may I call on you to settle?'

'At any time you wish,' Lucas said. 'I'll have the two thousand ready in cash.'

Enzo could not believe his ears. This was a Greek

and all Greeks were tricky, but in the ordinary way they weren't also mad. And that was what this action was. To try to twist a man like Enzo was an act of simple, staring lunacy.

Enzo said quietly: 'Within two days. And the sum agreed was *three* thousand pounds.'

Rex Lucas hung up. It was all in hand. Already his suave and well-dressed young man, the one he used to run his errands, would be talking to Michael Horan smoothly.

Despite the smoothness Horan had loathed him since his manner had been the purest establishment, and if you had to concede such men a virtue it was the fact they were mostly incorruptible. They therefore shouldn't be working for Lucas as the young man had promptly made clear he was. He had sent in his card, engraved impeccably, with his name and that of a rather grand club, then followed it up very smartly dressed—expensive linen and beautiful shoes.

'I'm calling for a friend in common. I believe you know Rex Lucas, don't you?'

'I've never met Mr Lucas in person.' Mike was thinking that this authentic exquisite was somehow letting his side down shamefully. Whatever else you might think of privilege you recognized that it held an advantage. Its owner could find work quite easily, an honest and often a fruitful job. It followed he shouldn't demean himself by scavenging for a scoundrel like Lucas, and clearly this man was doing just that.

'I think when you do you will rather like him.'

'I've an excellent reason to do the opposite.'

'So?' If the young man knew of Michael's beating

he did not betray the fact by a flicker. 'I've worked for him for some time myself and I've always found him perfectly reasonable.' He offered a cigarette and lit one. 'You will have gathered Rex Lucas would like to meet you.'

'I had gathered that from his sending a messenger.'

If the young man was piqued he hid it successfully, indeed he threw the word back adroitly. 'The message is for an early meeting.'

'Do you know what about?'

'I've a general idea.' He held his hand up as Horan started to speak. 'But no authority to discuss the details. In any case Lucas will do that better.'

'That's a bit of a pig in a poke.'

'Not quite. There's a matter between you which has been in dispute. Mr Lucas now thinks you can settle it amicably.'

Mike Horan thought it over carefully. This could hardly be another beating, for if violence were in Lucas's mind it would be possible just as much in Westercombe as it was by calling him up to London. Two approaches in one day—it was ominous. But whatever this one turned out to be it could hardly be more offensive than Charlotte's.

'When is this meeting suggested?'

'Early. At your convenience of course, but early.'

'Would tomorrow do?'

'That's very kind.'

When the young man had left Michael sent a telegram; he sent it to Mr Paul Martiny at *The Doelen* hotel in Amsterdam. Aunt Lilian had died in her sleep and he had decided to return to London on business which might turn out to be interesting.

14

Paul Martiny had had no doubts at all that he could do what he wished to in Amsterdam. He slipped dubious money outside the country and occasionally he would handle stones. So naturally he had some unusual contacts and one of them was Mijnheer Jos Visser. In Holland the name could also be Jewish but the Mijnheer was solidly, splendidly Dutch, blue-eyed and broad-shouldered, reassuringly Friesland.

He would have been horrified to be called a fence and indeed he was no such thing—far from it. When Martiny dealt in stolen stones, or stones, he thought smiling, which he guessed to be stolen, his market was Tel Aviv, not Holland, and the price he expected correspondingly lower. For Jos Visser was a respectable dealer. Where he differed from the run of the market was in a tolerant view of a diamond's provenance. He knew that the English had very strange laws, including Estate Duties at monstrous rates, and if heirs and sometimes legal executors found a way to avoid these outrageous charges a good capitalist's view would be sympathetic. He would wish to reassure himself that the stone he was buying wasn't dangerously hot, then he'd offer a little below its value, the shortfall on the market price representing the cost of a certain doubt. Not as to the seller's title—Jos Visser sent thieves about their business—but a doubt as to whether the man who offered had discharged all his fiscal debts in England. That wasn't a matter which troubled Jos

Visser, he wasn't within that jurisdiction, and if he could buy below the market he was a very happy man to do so.

Paul Martiny sometimes dealt with fences, though the bigger ones used much grander titles, but he saw no need to do so now. He had arranged an appointment and he walked in composedly; he showed the Dutchman aunt Lilian's pendant.

'Yours?' Visser asked.

'It is not.'

'Is it stolen?'

'If it were I wouldn't be coming to you.'

Jos Visser laughed: the answer pleased him. He had made his own discreet inquiries and he knew on whom else in other cities this Englishman had been known to call.

'Tell me the story,' he said.

Paul told him. He told him the whole story simply.

Jos Visser lit an East Indian cheroot, offering one to Paul Martiny. 'One or two questions. You do not mind?'

'Of course I don't mind. Please ask your questions.'

'Who else besides yourself now knows? I mean that these diamonds even exist. I do not count that bank of yours. I have dealt with them and fully trust them.'

'No one. Not even Michael Horan, though naturally I am going to tell him.'

The Dutchman didn't comment on this. He was a very good judge of men—he had need to be—and his instinct was that Martiny was truthful, but if an Englishman wished to swindle another that was something he would wish to keep out of. But why mention an heir of any sort if you intended to pocket the

139

proceeds yourself? Why not simply say you *were* the heir? Jos Visser had heard that tale before and twice he had declined to believe it. His feeling was that Martiny was straight but he was very Dutch and by nature cautious. He looked down at the diamonds and then at Paul.

'You told me where you found these and how.' He was thinking that if Martiny was lying it was an unnecessarily complex story. 'Do you wish to add to that?'

'No. Nothing.'

'And the old lady, you said, died the day before yesterday?'

'That you can of course check easily.'

Jos Visser blew smoke at the fine coffered ceiling; he looked down at the diamonds again and smiled. 'I am ready to do business,' he said. He was stoutish but had beautiful hands and he picked up the pendant and let it run through them. A low sun came through the open window and the stones were a stream of sinful fire.

'No need to doubt those,' Martiny said.

'I do not doubt them.'

Paul Martiny considered. 'They're of excellent size.'

The Dutchman smiled, he had read Paul's mind. Small stones could not be cut again; small stones could therefore be sometimes identified.

'I do not intend to recut these beauties.' He was emphatic, suddenly almost angry. 'I am a dealer in stones but I am not a barbarian. Of course I shall run no avoidable risks; I shall not attempt to sell this pendant, or not in the form which we see today. But the stones are much too fine to desecrate.' He looked at Paul Martiny again. 'Your price, if you please.'

Paul had it worked out, he knew the form. He knew the price of these diamonds if sold in Bond Street and the price they would fetch in Tel Aviv if they thought they were stolen and he couldn't disprove it. Somewhere between these two figures was Visser's. 'Three hundred thousand pounds,' he said.

Jos Visser shook his head at once. 'A proper price to start with, please.'

'Your turn, I think.'

'Two hundred thousand.'

They chaffered for half an hour in amity. Paul didn't think as Horan had that Dutchmen offered too little and asked too much. Perhaps it was true but what of that? They had other and compensatory virtues. Jos Visser, if he made a bargain, would carry it out without question or quibble.

At the end of half an hour's hard bargaining which Jos Visser enjoyed and Paul didn't resent they settled at two thirty-five thousand. The Dutchman didn't need paper and pencil, he worked it out in his head correctly. 'At the middle rate of exchange today that's a million four hundred and forty-three thousand. Gulden, of course.' He produced a cheque book. 'Have you a bank here?'

Paul named one he sometimes used.

'Excellent. That is also mine.' Jos Visser wrote the cheque and offered it.

'I'll take this down to our bank and pay it in.'

Jos Visser asked gently: 'To whose account?'

'To the account of Mr Michael Horan.'

'Very proper indeed.'

141

'What on earth can you mean?' Paul Martiny was very close to offence.

But the Dutchman raised a hand in peace. 'You must not misunderstand me, sir. I have trusted you, believed your story. If I had not done so I would not have bought from you.' He leant forward across the mahogany desk, amiable but also formidable. 'But I'm a man in a very delicate business and I have to take what are sane precautions. The moment you leave this office of mine I shall telephone to our mutual bank. Partly this is on your behalf. A million and a half is a substantial sum and a foreigner, even one they know, might raise eyebrows by paying it over the counter. But partly it's also a form of insurance.' He bowed formally, very Dutch indeed. 'You've been speaking of the man Michael Horan as the person who is really entitled, so if the money had gone in another name my cheque would have been stopped on the spot.' Visser added with his most peaceable smile: 'Would you not do the same, my friend?'

Paul Martiny thought it over, then laughed. 'You're a pleasure to do business with.'

'I hope to do business again.'

Paul caught the early flight next morning and drove straight from the airport to Michael Horan's. 'How's business?' he asked. 'The one in your telegram.'

'It hasn't developed yet but it will. I'm going to see Rex Lucas at noon.' Horan spoke with a sort of frozen calm which in any other circumstances would have frightened Paul Martiny severely, but today he bore

142

news, or believed he did, which would close this tiresome business finally.

'Rex Lucas? You can spit in his eye. You own two hundred and thirty-five thousand pounds.' As Horan started to speak Paul Martiny stopped him. 'I can make the story short and sweet. I told you once that if things came out right we should hold four aces and maybe the joker. Well, they did come out right —very right indeed. I did find aunt Lilian's diamonds hidden, and knowing you wouldn't want them as stones I took them to Amsterdam and sold them. You can pay Rex Lucas and walk away, and it'll still be a pretty rich man who does so. As for that Will you can afford to forget it. Apart from the diamonds aunt Lilian had little—I can't tell you how I know but I do. I should let the Telliers prove their Will, and a very unpleasant shock it will give them. A few thousand pounds less expenses of Probate. The real spoils are in your name in a bank. And nobody knows a thing but you and me. You follow what *that* means? You'd be a fool to pay Duty.'

Horan had risen while Paul was talking, pacing the room but not interrupting. Finally he sat down again. 'Any thanks I can offer sound simply absurd.'

'I don't want any thanks whatever, I merely did what I thought was right. Some people would say I've no moral sense, but I do have a pretty strong sense of family and I don't like people who bully old ladies.'

'You're a very strange man,' Mike Horan said.

'Perhaps I am but I've come to terms with it. In a different way you're unusual too. If you want to repay me you'll just act sensibly. Just pay Lucas his money and leave it be. God knows you can very well afford it.' Paul pulled out the cheque book. 'Here you are. I've even ventured to make out the cheque for you. Twenty-two thousand English pounds is a hundred and thirty-five thousand guilders. All you need do is sign at the bottom and throw it in Rex Lucas's face.'

'I'll do that with pleasure if he just doesn't lean on me.'

'I don't like the sound of that at all.'

'You know what I am.'

'And I know what you're not. You're behaving like a Spanish nobleman and a pretty old-fashioned *hidalgo* at that.' Paul was conscious of a real disappointment. This man was hopeless, you couldn't help him. Knowing it sounded weak he said: 'Keep me in touch with what happens, please.'

'I certainly owe you that. I promise.'

'Then I'll be driving down to the country at once.'

Paul collected his car with a sense of annoyance. God dammit he'd gone to a deal of trouble, God dammit the affair should be over. With any normal man it would be. A sensible one wouldn't even see Lucas, he'd put the cheque in the post and go his way. But Horan had been summoned peremptorily and it was Paul's strong impression he'd greatly resented it. So he'd go to Rex Lucas to see what he'd say, put the whole affair in the balance again against the irrelevant weight of how Lucas behaved to him. With fools the gods themselves fought helplessly.

But as he drew nearer his home his spirits rose. He needed the escape and spur of managing the affairs of criminals under his cover of a Bleeding Heart, but he owned three thousand fertile acres and took pride in the fact that he farmed them profitably. He hadn't at this moment of time any criminal with a pressing problem, but the next four weeks of a farmer's year were always very busy ones and he wouldn't be feeling the need to escape.

And he was looking forward to seeing his wife. They didn't sleep together now but Paul Martiny would never change her. He grinned as a mental ear caught sharply the exact tone of her warm but placid greeting. 'Where have you been?' A simple question. No hint of annoyance or disapproval. Pussy cat, pussy cat, where have you been? So 'I've been in Amsterdam,' he would say, and Matilda Martiny's face wouldn't change. She wasn't in the very least stupid, she knew all about Amsterdam by hearsay. She'd assume he'd been beating around its brothels, but she wouldn't move a muscle assuming it. She'd have a basket on her arm with roses and later she would bring him a gin. She was dotty on genealogy and sometimes she was a bit of a snob but he wouldn't change the old bag for the mines of the Rand.

And certainly not for mere adventure, like involving himself with Michael Horan. He'd decided by now that he'd done so in anger. Both of them had a common enemy, the conventional, crumbling world around them, but to act in anger was always dangerous, especially with a man like Horan. Horan had been to prison: Paul had not. Nevertheless he might one day do so if he let his emotions rule his head. Thinking coolly as he drove to his home he decided he'd seen the last of Horan.

He drove up the modest drive and stopped. Matilda Martiny emerged from the hall.

'Where have you been?'

'In Amsterdam.'

She had a basket on her arm with roses.

'Then I'll get you a gin. You can probably use it.'

He drank it in peace, his tension relaxed. He had done what he thought right. It was finished. He hadn't a further obligation. Horan had promised to ring again if anything went wrong.

It wouldn't.

15

Rex Lucas's official religion was that of the Greek Orthodox church, for though he had long been settled in England no church would have appealed to him whose traditional and triumphant credo was the song entitled The Vicar of Bray. So when Rex Lucas crossed himself, an action he indulged in seldom, he did it the wrong way round, like a Greek. This, then, was his official religion which he showed on such forms as required him to do so, but at heart, like many Greeks from the country, he had kept a streak of ancestral paganism. He needn't walk far from his native village, up to the stony but beautiful hills, before he'd find a shrine his blood would recognize, crumbling now and often hidden, but still with the proud and classic symbol, often a chaplet of flowers to wreath it. Sometimes he'd see a girl from the village, shyly retreating but not in shame, knowing this god would find her a lover when the men in black robes with uncomely beards found her nothing but a dour frustration.

But these gods would be roaring Olympic laughter when their Messenger brought them the news of Rex Lucas. Rex Lucas was destroying himself and his end would encompass an Attic tragedy. Whom the gods destroy they first drive mad? Not that since they'd never heard of Lucas; he wasn't big enough to invite destruction. But there was a *hubris* about this mortal clown and no Greek be he mortal or pagan god's ghost could resist the appeal of a classic irony.

For Rex Lucas was in a deadly temper. Enzo's manner on the telephone had been a warning which he couldn't ignore. Lucas wasn't in his way insensitive but still he hankered to cheat the Sicilian, driven by the blind compulsion which made some men pick their steps between paving-stones. And he had better and more logical reason to feel that he was hardly used. Mike Horan owed him money, did he? He wasn't the only man who did so. Lucas could deal with Mike Horan and meant to, but he couldn't deal with Charles Desouter. Who had simply announced that he wouldn't pay, and if he had to resign from his club, well, it bored him. Moreover he was a Member of Parliament, one far to the Left and also unscrupulous. With such a man the frighteners were out of any practical question and anything more would be suicidal. If Lucas brought other pressures to bear Desouter would return them with interest. He wasn't a man of strict moral principle and he'd start rumours where they would really hurt.... Lucas's table were mostly straight, but occasionally, very occasionally indeed ... True or false the rumour would spread and it could shut Lucas down inside a month.

He snarled since he knew Desouter had beaten him. Then all the more reason that Horan shouldn't. Lucas looked forward to their appointment at noon for he believed that he knew how to deal with Horan.

If his ears had been something more than human they'd have picked up the echo of laughter above him.

Because Mike Horan had been thinking too and had decided that Paul's advice had been sound. Even to accept the risk that Lucas would start to lean on him was indefensible when you thought of it sensibly,

148

and moreover it was entirely unnecessary. So don't give him the chance to lean on you, just give him that cheque and walk away. Michael Horan had already signed it. But it was permissible to keep your appointment, to go to Rex Lucas in person and watch his face. Not to humiliate—that would be childish—but curiosity was in this case allowable, indeed one would have to be more than human just to put that cheque in Her Majesty's mail.

So he called at twelve o'clock precisely and immediately matters went sadly wrong. Not for Horan but for Lucas upstairs, who knew nothing of diamonds or guilders or cheques on them. He had arranged Mike's reception with a good deal of care, ignorant that in the altered circumstances that reception was the worst one possible.

It began when Horan rang the bell at the fine Victorian house in Belgravia. The square was still well-preserved and prosperous, the ambience one of business societies and the embassies of second league Powers. Into this air of solid correctitude a top class casino blended comfortably, but not the way it received Mike Horan. He had expected a butler; he did not find one. Instead a man in shirtsleeves grinned at him, not hurrying to let him pass. Michael had seen him before and remembered him. He had a great deal of hair in front of his ears and mean pig's eyes in a pasty face. Another reason Michael remembered him was that he'd suffered at his hands severely. The man stood in the door and sneered at him. 'I know you,' he said. 'We've met before.'

Mike Horan didn't answer this. He swallowed but somehow kept his hands still.

The man stood aside and bowed insultingly; he jerked a thumb at the staircase inside. 'Up there. You go first.'

'No thank you, I'll follow.' Mike didn't fancy this man behind him.

The strongarm hesitated but finally shrugged and they went up the stairs in single file. At the top they turned left where a door was open. The strongarm stood aside again. 'In there,' he said, and he pushed Horan violently. Michael didn't quite fall for he caught at a table. When he recovered the door had been shut on him. He tried it. It had been firmly locked.

He sat down on a sofa and looked around him. He was in some sort of ante-room, finely proportioned and better furnished. The pictures on the wall were hunting scenes with occasional portraits of nameless grandees. All one side of the room was a very long bar, now unattended and shuttered up. In another wall were sliding doors and Michael Horan decided to try them. To his surprise they moved and he looked through them curiously. This was one of several gaming-rooms—three tables, all for straight roulette. There were splendidly opulent chandeliers and more comfortable chairs around the tables than were found in many foreign casinos. At the last of the tables a man was working, dismounting the wheel to make some adjustment. Michael's first and very natural thought was that some croupier was busy fixing his wheel, but on reflection he turned it down as improbable. Of the various methods of cheating the gambler tilting the wheel was much the simplest, but it was also the least sophisticated, the most likely to be spotted quickly by any customer of modest experience. No, if the house were favoured in Lucas's gambling rooms it would be favoured by much less obvious means.

The man at the table ignored Mike Horan and for a moment he considered a dash for it. But this idea too he turned down on reflection. He had unfinished business to settle with Lucas and sometime he would have to do so. Moreover he'd been received with contumely, locked in alone and left to wait. The last thing he was going to do was to run away as though he'd been frightened.

He returned to his sofa and sat down quietly. There was nothing to read and Michael was bored. Also his bile was rising steadily. He looked at his watch—a full fifteen minutes. He would give them five more, then walk out through the gaming room. Probably someone would try to stop him and that would mean a disturbance, not business. But he wouldn't sit long with a door locked behind him. He dared not, he was getting angry, and anger was much the worst of his counsellors.

He counted five minutes away on his watch, then rose and walked to the sliding doors. As he did so he heard a key turn behind him. It was the Kraut with the pig's eyes and grinning again.

'Cooled your heels off a little?'

'I wasn't hot.'

... That wasn't a very effective comeback and also it wasn't entirely true. I am getting very hot indeed.

'The big boy is ready to see you. *Komm.*'

They went up another flight of stairs to another fine room at the top of the house. This was where

Lucas had entertained Paul, but normally it was used as his office. Now the furniture of a room of business was back in its place and looking formidable. Lucas himself sat behind the desk. He didn't rise as Horan came in nor offer him a chair to sit on.

'On the other side of the table. And listen.'

Michael hesitated but in the end moved slowly. The strongarm took up station behind him and a second man rose from a chair and joined him. He was a crophead whom Michael had not yet seen.

'Now,' Lucas said, 'you owe me money.'

It was on the tip of Horan's tongue to say: 'Yes, and I've come here today to pay it,' but the sentence was choked in his mouth unspoken. He didn't like standing before this man and he liked even less having thugs behind him.

'You are now in a position to pay me. You are the heir to a very large estate.'

'You mean my great aunt's, Lilian Gregg? I'm afraid you may be disappointed.'

For a moment Rex Lucas looked surprised but he recovered almost at once and asked:

'You've heard rumours about a different Will?'

Mike Horan didn't answer this.

'I asked you a question.'

'I've decided to answer it. I *have* heard various, varying rumours.'

'They are true but you may also forget them. The second Will was made under duress. Therefore it is entirely worthless. It could possibly have been challenged in any case, but now that its two witnesses have conveniently decided to die—what a fortunate young man you are!—it can be challenged with confident hope of success.'

'You're very well informed.'

'I need to be.'

'You're going to challenge this Will and restore the first one?'

'I have no standing. But *you* will challenge it. I will put you in funds to make that possible.'

'Very kind.'

'Plain business.'

Mike had forgotten the cheque in his pocket. He was fascinated: this man was fascinating. He was also on all the odds a killer. For twenty-two thousand pounds. Astonishing.

'Let me get this proposition straight. So I challenge the second Will and restore the first. Then I pay you what I owe you. Correct?'

'Not quite, I'm afraid. You also have to repay me the money which I shall lend you to conduct your case. There will further be the matter of interest since you've kept me out of my debt for some time. That will be at twenty per cent.'

'A year?'

'No, a month.'

At the end of a considerable silence Mike Horan said: 'I'll think it over.'

'You don't need to do that, I've arranged the whole matter. You have an appointment this afternoon with my lawyers. They know what to do—you instruct them formally.'

'I still think I'll think it over, though.'

'I was afraid you might say that.'

'Why afraid?'

'Because you're a very foolish man. What you suffered once you can suffer again. Again and again and worse and worse.'

'I think I could defend myself now you've given me such a friendly warning.'

Rex Lucas's eyes had begun to hood again. 'You're thinking of the men behind you?'

'Or others you may care to hire.'

'I can hire such men and I often do. Don't you ever see matters as two plus two? Don't you put them together and make them four?'

'In this case I'm fairly sure they're five.'

Rex Lucas began to repeat himself, speaking with deliberation. 'What a fortunate young man you are! Two witnesses have conveniently died.'

'I didn't miss that the first time you said it.'

'Then what did you make of it?'

'What I made of it isn't important now. What I make of it is very simple. You're threatening to kill me. Bluff.'

'Care to call it?'

'I intend to do so.'

Mike Horan had been increasingly scared that he'd lose his temper and do something foolish but it was Lucas whose temper cracked first and decisively. He stood up suddenly, banging the desk. His voice had blurred and his eyes looked sightless. To the men behind Horan he said:

'Throw him out. And in doing so teach him a serious lesson.'

They were on him before he could turn and defend himself, each taking an arm in an old-fashioned hammer lock. Old-fashioned, Mike Horan found time to reflect, but also extremely effective in hobbling him. Especially with a man on each arm. One could hold him while the other crippled him, raising the elbow and snapping the shoulder.

Instead they frogmarched him down the two flights of stairs and a third man appeared and opened the door to them. They balanced Michael on top of eight noble steps and one man began to raise his left arm. Michael went limp since he couldn't counter but the crophead settled the issue brutally. He kicked Michael between the lumbar vertebrae with the end of a wickedly steel-shod boot and Michael went down the steps arms flailing. He lay still at the bottom in bitter pain, but in the street they didn't dare follow it up. He heard a jeering laugh and a door slam viciously, then he picked himself up and walked stiff-legged till he found a cruising taxi and hailed it.

'Where to?' the driver asked.

'To Soho.'

Michael gave him the name of a little-known pub.

He sat back, eyes closed, fighting the pain, hoping his spine wasn't damaged permanently. Prison had taught him many things, most of them outside the curriculum, and one of them was the name of this pub.

Where you could usually buy some sort of gun if you looked all right and had it in cash.

Fat George had been having a good deal of trouble in selling Gilbert Heale-Mann's two-two. There was a heat on in the matter of firearms and the regular dealers had gone to ground. In theory this should have made it easier for a man who wasn't a regular dealer, but it had also frightened potential customers. Who weren't, as the Press often loudly asserted, the criminal class with an itch to kill, but mostly elderly and respectable people determined to defend themselves, more determined to defend their property against the outrage of having it smashed and ravaged by young savages who'd be better in labour camps. These were the people who came to this pub as the word passed discreetly from mouth to ear, but now the word was one of caution. Some official in the Home Office had put pressure on a senior policeman. The result, though it could hardly last, had been a slump in the market for all sorts of weapons.

So the pistol was still on Fat George's hands and he'd begun to despair of ever selling it, but when Mike Horan came in he had sensed at once that this was a potential customer. He was a good deal below the average age of people who wanted unlawful pistols—unlawful because they couldn't get licences, not unlawful because they'd neglected to try to—but perhaps he was a bachelor who lived alone with objects of value.

Horan went up to the bar and sat at it, ordering a large gin and tonic. He drank it and another one, then he turned on his stool and looked round the room. There was only one other man in it—George. He was sitting on a bench by the wall. Mike Horan had no instinct about him as Fat George had had about Mike Horan, but he knew that he'd have to take his chances and moreover he'd have to take them urgently. He had been fairly sure that Rex Lucas was bluffing, at any rate in the matter of killing him. A dead man couldn't dispute a Will. But if

Lucas had written off his money he might change the debt's form to Mike's very grave peril, and throwing him down his splendid steps suggested that he had done just that. It could then be a matter of Lucas's ethos, the compulsive urge for a new satisfaction. Most men would call it simply revenge.

So Mike climbed off his stool—his pain was diminishing—and came over to sit beside Fat George.

'I've a feeling we've met before.'

'It's possible.' George was civil but he wasn't forthcoming. He wasn't sure about Horan and he liked to be certain.

'At that conference.'

'Which one?'

'The one about selling ironmongery.'

'You are interested in ironmongery?'

'Certain sorts of ironmongery.'

Fat George considered it very carefully. He needed the money, he needed it badly. Lucas wasn't now giving him regular work and his other sources of income were fragile. He said so the barman shouldn't hear him:

'I'm going to the loo. Alone. Give me a minute then follow me naturally.'

Horan gave him his minute, then followed him in. Fat George produced the two-two and showed it. 'With twenty-five slugs,' he said. 'A hundred.'

Mike Horan was disappointed and showed it. He knew little of guns but he knew enough. In the hands of a man who was good with pistols this toy was as lethal as anything bigger, but Mike Horan had never fired a pistol. He didn't want to kill a man, or not unless he was finally forced to; he wanted to stop him doing him mayhem and for that he needed a stopping weapon.

But he took the gun and examined it carefully, noting that George had kept it well. It was better than nothing.

'I'll give you fifty.'

Fat George took the gun back at once and pocketed it. This didn't run to form, it looked odd. He would have sold the pistol for fifty pounds to a man he felt was entirely genuine, but this looked suspicious, it wasn't right. Horan's age apart, and that was wrong too, customers who wanted weapons mostly paid what they were asked without quibble. If they knew enough to come to this pub they would also know the going rate. They paid in old notes with elastic bands round them, money which they could ill afford but which foolish laws and more foolish magistrates forced them to squander in self defence.

'I'll make it sixty,' Horan said.

'No deal. Not to you. At any price.'

'You suspect that I'm not what I seem?'

'It's possible.'

'I assure you I'm not a plain clothes Jack, but if you think I am of course that ends it. Good morning to you and thanks for the offer.'

Mike took another taxi home and as he got out he met the General. The last time he'd seen him he had looked very ill but now he was looking a great deal worse. He was still well turned out and as tidy as ever but his skin looked taut and grey and old and as he faced Horan he slightly staggered. He's been lunching too well at his club, Michael thought, and indeed there was a smell of drink.

The General said: 'You've been away.'

'I've been down in the West Country a bit.'

'I hope you enjoyed it.'

'Not entirely.'

'I haven't been enjoying life either. Since you weren't around you won't have heard.' The General straightened his back. 'My wife died three days ago.'

'I'm very sorry,' Michael said. It sounded quite absurdly inadequate.

'You needn't be that—it was a happy release. I dare say you guessed what she had. It was terminal. Two operations and that was the end of it.' Even now that she was dead and buried the General couldn't bring himself to utter the appalling word. 'I had to watch it and it broke me up. I look at myself in the glass and see it. And thank you again for your splendid doctor. The other man followed some crazy religion; he really believed that suffering was good for you.' The old man snorted in grim contempt. 'I will bet he had never seen a battlefield. He gave my wife something but not enough. Not strong enough and not enough. Damn his soul. But your man saw her out in peace. He shortened her life by perhaps a fortnight, he was that sort of doctor and not a coward.' The General gave Michael a look of apology. 'I've been talking too much. I beg your pardon.'

Michael had been thinking humbly. This old man was sick and broken and lonely. 'Would you like to talk some more? It might help.' He could talk at his club, Michael guessed, but not this way. It wouldn't be done, they would all edge away from him.

159

The General seemed uncertain, then nodded. 'You're very kind. I'd like to do that.'

They went upstairs to Horan's flat where the General had never been before. Michael gave him a chair and a very large whisky.

'The first today,' the General said. 'For forty-eight hours after Flora died I kept myself as tight as a fart, then I realized it was getting me nowhere. But there was some stuff left from what your doctor gave her. He made me promise to return what was left. After Flora went out, I mean. I didn't. I'm ashamed to say I have broken a promise.'

Mike Horan cut down an audible whistle. He could guess at one drug which this stuff might be, and with alcohol and an ageing man it was something which could be as deadly as arsenic. He looked at the whisky. The General had called it the first of the day but Michael had very good reason to doubt him. In the street the old man had staggered noticeably, almost as though he were walking in sleep. Well, there it was, it wasn't Mike's business; he could hardly snatch the whisky back because an unhappy old man was ashamed of his drinking.

But the General had started to talk again. 'It's funny how marriages start and end. I didn't intend to marry Flora but Flora intended to marry me. We had a couple of boys who were both of them killed. In 'forty-two on Kidney Ridge. And that was the end of it.' He added with an apparent inconsequence. 'Poor Flora could never get things right, not the time or the bills or the laundry or anything. In middle life she was hell to live with and there were times I could have killed her cheerfully. But then, I don't

160

know, we both grew older, used to each other—in some ways dependent. Now I miss her very much indeed.' The General looked shyly at Michael Horan. 'I'll tell you the truth and it's very simple. I don't want to go on living without her.'

Michael Horan wasn't embarrassed by this, it was said too simply and clearly true, but he didn't know what to reply so kept silent. Presently he asked the General:

'Would you care for another drink?'

'I thank you.'

Michael had decided by now that the General had probably had his ration so the whisky he poured was distinctly smaller. It was, that is, when he started to pour it, but in the mirror he caught the old man's eye. It wasn't in any way disapproving but there was a glint in it which might be amusement. Horan doubled the dose and brought it over.

'That's a very large drink.'

'But you won't refuse it.'

'I shall certainly do no such thing.' The General put it down in three, then he rose to his feet. He was now pretty shaky.

'I've been a terrible bore.' His voice had thickened.

'I doubt if you could ever be that.'

'Then I'm going to impose on your kindness again. I'm lonely as I told you—unhappy.' The last word came out with a sort of slurred stutter. 'If you should ever be able to spare a moment, would you come up and talk to me? I know it's a lot to ask—'

'I'd like to.'

The old man straightened again, then made an uncertain way to the door. At it he gave Michael a

161

key. 'I only bolt myself in at night. That was one of the things which Flora hated—all these ruffians about I can hardly blame her. The cleaning woman could lose her key and then we might get unwelcome visitors. But I still keep a very effective deterrent.'

The General went out and Michael sat down again to consider a remarkable day. But he found that he couldn't focus his thinking. Something was nagging, inhibiting thought. It wasn't pity for a brave old man nor a feeling of self-congratulation that a guess of his had once been right: like many of his age and background the General did keep a gun around him. Presently it came to him; he was under an obligation, a promise. He had promised to keep Paul Martiny informed if anything went awry. As it had. Rex Lucas had done more than lean on him, he'd used contemptuous violence and threats for the future. Mike Horan suspected he wouldn't kill him, a stiff couldn't go to a court for Probate, but the other threat had been very real. Those men could come round at any time and he hadn't succeeded in finding a weapon. He needn't tell this to Paul and alarm him and he'd been prevented by force from acting foolishly, but the fact remained that he hadn't paid Lucas. The cheque Paul had written was still in his pocket.

Paul Martiny wouldn't like that in the least but Horan had given a formal promise.

He rang up Martiny and caught him at home. 'Michael Horan here. It all went wrong. The talk with Rex Lucas, I mean. The whole thing.'

Martiny said wearily: 'So he leant on you and you lost your temper. You did something stupid—'

'I did nothing whatever. I was received with two

hoodlums behind my back. Later they threw me down the steps.'

'Literally?'

'Very literally. Yes.'

Paul Martiny didn't believe what he heard. It sounded an utterly pointless and futile action. 'After paying him his money? Why?'

'I didn't pay him any money. Why should I? You said it yourself. He leant on me.'

'But he must have made some proposition.'

'I was to challenge the second Will—he'd finance it. Then I was to pay with the proceeds plus interest at an iniquitous rate.'

'If you hadn't paid him off already that was the moment to pull that cheque out.'

Mike Horan didn't answer; he hadn't one.

Paul Martiny asked with increasing anger: 'So what's going to happen now?'

'I don't know. But he said he'd repeat the previous treatment unless I did what he said and started a law suit.'

'So we're back to Square One and the hoodlums you talked about. Living in constant fear or running away. You spoke of the West Indies once—'

'I'm not going to run away from Lucas.'

'What will you do?'

'I'll see it out.'

'You're a bloody fool.' Martiny rang off. He was a very disappointed man.

16

It had not been Rex Lucas's lucky day. He wasn't always greedy and stupid, conditioned by inherited avarice. If he had been he couldn't have built an empire, the dominion of a chain of high class casinos with all the trapping of dubious power which went with it—an informer in a firm of solicitors, men like Fat George who would seek and find for him, frighteners and brutal bullies, the smooth young man to grease costive wheels. By the time he had eaten his lunch he was sane again, knowing he'd handled Horan badly but in no way inclined to rescind his instructions. That he could never do: his blood was Greek. In Byzantium face had been all important.

But Enzo was a different matter and Enzo was coming that afternoon. It was earlier than Lucas had expected his call, but he had made up his conscious and thinking mind; he'd play fair with this Sicilian since a thousand pounds saved was not worth trouble. He had decided this as a matter of business, though Enzo diminished his ego severely, he made him feel small, stole his hard-won assurance. Money to a man like Enzo was something you earned to live well and fully, and if you earned it by killing other men you were still an unbridgeable gulf apart from another who earned it by taking percentages. It didn't matter how large the percentage was, how great was the fortune salted away in numbered accounts and discreet bars of bullion. You were a tradesman still and no money could change it. Enzo had never said such a thing but Lucas knew perfectly well that he thought it.

When Enzo arrived he was greeted with ceremony —no strongarms, no kicking his heels in a waiting-room but the smooth young man at the door in person. He greeted Enzo by his style and title for he was the sort of young man who looked such things up.

'I haven't called myself that for many years. Just call me Signor Enzo, please.'

'Certainly Signor. Please come with me.'

They went upstairs, this time in a lift, upholstered in buttoned leather, flashy. In Lucas's room he rose at once, offering a chair and whisky. Enzo took the chair, declined the whisky. The smooth young man bowed to both and slid out.

'A successful conclusion,' Lucas said.

'I had rather more luck that I'd really hoped for.'

'You do not mind a business question?'

'I do not mind it. I may not answer.' The voice hadn't changed, it was still cool and courteous, but the snub had been abrasive and final. Lucas almost held his question back but he was worried and worry wrecked his sleep. He went at it crabwise, excessively Greek.

'You explained to me once—let us call them your principles. To qualify as an artistic killing that killing must look like an accident. Yes? And presumably it must stay that way.'

'Perfectly correct. I did say that.'

'Which that doctor's death will presumably do, or at worst we can hope for no more than suspicion.

But in the case of the man Heale-Mann—'

Enzo laughed. It was an acid and ironic sound, the sound of a man who had seen through his questioner and who knew his motives and read his fears. Rex Lucas had now been snubbed twice; he was furious. His good intentions, his sensible thinking, were fading under the lash of contempt.

But Enzo was going on again, impersonal and therefore insulting. 'I can save you expressing your question in terms. Killing that lawyer was also an accident, or rather it will look like one. Temporarily. After that there will be a hue and cry and it's possible it will end up at my door. But you may take it I've worked out my margin of time. I've enough but not a great deal to play with.'

'You have?' Lucas asked. He had to be sure.

'My plane leaves tomorrow at half past one.'

'But suppose they try for extradition?'

Enzo thought it a very foolish question. He couldn't live in mainland Italy but then he wasn't a mainland Italian. In Palermo he was highly respected, he knew the ropes and how to use them. He knew who to sweeten and how to do it, he had a niece who had married a senior policeman, a daughter betrothed to a politician. He had made the *combinazioni* without which a Sicilian's life could be dangerous. Enzo said coldly:

'I can mind my own business. Which word reminds me. I have called on you for the fee you owe me.'

Rex Lucas had been slipping fast. He had determined that morning that he'd play this one honestly, but now he hated this man and resented his patronage. And Enzo had made an unnoticed mistake—unnoticed by him but not by Lucas. He was leaving at half past one tomorrow. It was now half past four in the afternoon.

... He won't dare delay it, his margin won't let him.

Rex Lucas passed over two thousand pounds, two piles of a thousand each in rubber bands.

Enzo stared at them, his face expressionless. There were several things he could do; he considered them. He could protest, which he turned down at once. It was undignified and it would also be futile: this man had made his foolish choice and he wouldn't be moved by any words. Or he could pick up the money and throw it at Lucas. A gesture of contempt no doubt, but also melodramatic and profitless. Enzo wasn't in need of two thousand pounds, he had a villa and some fertile land, brothels in cities in mainland Italy, and some establishments in his native island which earned even more than well run bordellos. But one didn't play into an enemy's hands by offering a romantic gesture and leaving him laughing his devious face off. Enzo picked up the money and counted it carefully.

'One thousand short,' he said at last.

'The sum agreed was four thousand pounds. Two on the first of two occurrences and two when you completed the second.'

'My recollection of that is different.'

'Your recollection is also mistaken.'

Enzo wasn't greatly interested in the psychology of a man he despised. He had decided that Lucas was simply stupid and for the moment that was more than enough. For a gambler he read odds very badly. It was foolish to lay a rich man's life against a matter of a thousand pounds.

'I will call again at noon tomorrow to receive from you one thousand pounds.'

Rex Lucas simply shrugged and rose.

Enzo rose too; he didn't seem angry, and Lucas, if he'd known more of Latins, would have seen that as the most urgent warning. He had expected protest and probably bluster, so this fatalistic acquiescence he read as a saving of face—no more. Enzo must know that his chances were nil. He hadn't the time to set up any chance, so he was making a gesture to save his dignity.

Enzo said coldly: 'Don't show me out.'

'As you please.'

Rex Lucas was feeling on top again and as a Greek he overplayed his hand. He risked a sarcasm and it cost him his life. 'It's been a pleasure to do business with you.'

Enzo didn't answer him. He opened the door for himself in silence. He found his way out, looking sharply around him, especially at the splendid staircase. A man trapped in a lift was entirely defenceless.

Enzo memorized the layout precisely.

Mike Horan woke the following morning after a restless and unrestoring night. Two deathsheads had grinned, one each end of his pillow, competing for his reluctant attention. The first reminded Michael sourly that he still had no weapon of any kind, and Horan didn't doubt for a moment that Rex Lucas would be as bad as his word. Sooner or later, probably sooner, there'd be another beating, perhaps a snatch, and this time it might be more than just pressure. If Lucas had written his money off, and his actions had suggested he had, the strongarms who called would have fresh instructions. They wouldn't be trying to force him to payment but simply to exact revenge. And that could be worse, very seriously worse, than any routine but still limited beating. With a man like Rex Lucas you could never be sure. With megalomaniacs nobody could be, and Mike Horan had a disquieting suspicion that easy affluence and the power to buy violence had infected Rex Lucas with a dangerous illusion. It was the illusion that he possessed real power, that money was above the law. And Rex Lucas had made a great deal of money.

The second deathshead had been slightly less menacing since its warning had been for another man. Michael Horan was anxious about the old General, a man to whom he owed the fact that he hadn't been sent to a glasshouse and broken. He had looked very ill when he'd seen him last and he'd admitted to two days' heavy drinking immediately after the death of his wife. He had said that it had got him nowhere, implying that he had cut down on the bottle, but Horan wasn't convinced he had. His speech had been passably close to normal, but he had staggered more than once, almost fallen, and he'd said something about what he'd called some stuff. Apparently it had helped him. No doubt. It had been treatment for a dying woman, one dying in unbearable pain, and though Michael Horan knew nothing of pharmacy he read his daily newspaper and he knew that there was more than one drug which with alcohol could be quietly lethal. Of course it was the General's life, not a happy one and not much remaining. All the more reason to smooth what was left of it. The General had admitted loneliness, an appeal which from a man of his type was as mandatory as a scream in the night. He'd even given Mike Horan a key.

Mike Horan slipped upstairs and used it. There was nobody in the sitting-room, and Michael, who'd never been in it, looked round him. The aura was unmistakably military—the stuffed heads of unknown beasts on the walls, the group photographs and old firearms crossed, a tiger skin on the parquet floor. To the left of the door was a glass-topped case and Michael Horan glanced in it hurriedly. It was crammed with medals and various Orders. Michael knew that the General was very well decorated but he could hardly have earned this collection himself. Most of them Michael had never seen but two he had and they weren't earned easily. The rest must go back the best part of a century, at least three generations of men, an unprofitable but still splendid heritage of lives spent in service if not always intelligently.

Michael called softly: 'General. General.'

Nobody answered. He went to the bedroom.

His first feeling was one of extreme embarrassment, for the old man was on the bed, fully dressed. Michael looked at his watch: it was half past nine. Men of a military background rose early, so the General, last night, had taken a skinful and dropped on his bed to sleep it off. Michael Horan turned to tiptoe out but some instinct began to clamour insistently. There was something in the way the man lay ...

Horan went to the bed and called again. 'General.' The old man on the bed didn't wake or stir. Michael felt for his pulse and didn't find it. He fetched a shaving mirror and held it up; he held it before the General's mouth. The mirror stayed entirely unclouded. On the bedside table was a bottle of whisky. There was only a tot or two left. That said little. No hypodermic or drug was visible. And that in turn said nothing whatever. An inquest might have to decide all that.

Horan went to the phone to ring the doctor. Whether he also called the police was a matter this doctor would have to decide, but Michael felt fairly sure he would not. So he picked up the phone but put it down again. He couldn't recall his doctor's number but it was written in his address book downstairs.

He went to the door but froze suddenly, silent. He could see down the stairs to his own front door and two men were breaking into his flat. One was Crophead, the other the smooth young man.

Michael slid back behind the door. It was the ease of it which astonished and shocked him. They weren't fiddling with skeleton keys, they were simply cutting the lock out bodily. The young man was putting away a drill having made two neat holes at a six-inch interval. Crophead was using a thin steel saw, cutting once to the left, then downwards, then left again. When he'd finished they simply pushed the door open. The lock fell to the ground and they picked it up.

Michael Horan went back to the General's living-room. He'd confirmed to him only the day before that he did keep what he'd called a deterrent, and Michael needed to find it quickly.

He found it almost at once, without difficulty, in a

drawer of the desk in its canvas holster. Michael Horan took it out and looked at it. It was the reverse of what Fat George had offered him, a formidable Service weapon which would stop any man alive in his tracks even if it only wounded him. It was beautifully kept as though for inspection and at the back of the drawer was a box of cartridges. Michael loaded the pistol and stood back, balancing it. In his army days he'd fired various firearms but of hand guns he had had no experience. What had been the doctrine then, what had they once casually told him? Revolvers weren't private soldiers' weapons, but if ever you should find yourself with a pistol and nothing else in the world, remember that you weren't in a Western. No fancy shooting—no indeed. You held the thing in both hands and pulled; you went on pulling till the other man dropped.

Michael snapped the revolver shut and checked the safety. Then he went silently down to his flat.

That morning Paul Martiny too had woken after a restless night. Nobody had been threatening him, he hadn't any private worries for sad old men who might do something foolish. Nevertheless he had slept very badly.

He decided over his morning tea that what had ruined his night was a sense of inadequacy, a feeling he hadn't completed a duty. All logic and common sense said he had, but logic and sense were for once unconvincing. He'd involved himself in Mike Horan's affairs for reasons which might not stand up to questioning but to Paul they'd been strong and he didn't regret them. Michael Horan was his sort of

172

man. Paul could have been a Horan himself if he hadn't been born to a modest privilege, to the protection of an established order. Which he despised and secretly flouted outrageously. So he'd liked Michael Horan and even admired him, and there was the factor that he was being swindled. But no, Paul couldn't lean hard on that. It was true he had a sense of family but it was a realistic one and sensibly limited. He had had to ask a half-German wife what relationship he bore to Horan, and it hadn't in any normal sense been much more than a name on a family tree. But old Lilian Gregg had been more important. He'd looked up to her as a splendid survival and they'd been bullying her in a Home for the Elderly. Paul Martiny wouldn't tolerate that. What had started as a casual sympathy for a man he had liked but to whom he owed nothing had ended in a deep involvement.

So Paul Martiny had helped Mike Horan and far beyond what he'd first intended. He had found aunt Lilian's diamonds for him and sold them well in Amsterdam. For the first time that morning Martiny smiled. That had been good, it had cocked a snook, like secretly managing criminals' money. The stones' proceeds were now in a solid Dutch bank and a country which he'd begun to hate would see not a penny in wicked Duty.

All this, then, was good. Was it good enough? Paul had begun to think it wasn't. Mike Horan had rung him and Paul had been furious. It had been one thing to respect a man, quite another to involve himself further when that man showed a dangerous bloody-mindedness. But hadn't Paul always known he would do so, hadn't he always thought of him as a hair-trigger man who'd go off if you shook him? So again with fools the gods were powerless. True. But Paul Martiny wasn't a god, he was a man who had made a conscious decision to help a man for whom he'd felt sympathy.

Who'd now put himself in a hopeless position. He had said that he'd been threatened again, and though Patíl had only met Lucas once he didn't believe that he'd threaten idly. No doubt he bluffed wildly, most Greeks did that, but he had given one reason for violent action which to Paul Martiny was wholly convincing. He couldn't let Horan off his hook when by going to the courts he could pay him. Mike Horan, who'd once been a simple bilker, someone you frightened and later beat, had challenged Rex Lucas head on, his whole system.

... Another establishment. Christ, how I loathe them.

Then bring him down to the country and hide him? That was on—Paul could do it. He had a cottage which at this moment was empty and a farm hand who had once been a wrestler. He could shack them up together....

It wouldn't do, it was only temporary. With all that beautiful money in Holland Michael Horan wouldn't stay long in the country and he'd insisted he wasn't inclined to run for it. He was a man of the cities and to a town he'd return. Where Rex Lucas, who could clearly arrange things, would be tempted to arrange again.

Paul Martiny got up and made more tea. He never woke Matty to do it for him, she hated to be woken early. Then he bathed and shaved and dressed himself quickly. He took his car and drove fast to London. He hadn't even the ghost of a plan, he was going to play this one by ear. But he'd have to call in on Mike Horan at once for he was still in the game and he couldn't cut out of it.

17

Martiny had found the front door ajar and he came up the stairs to Mike Horan's flat as Michael was creeping down from the General's. He started to speak but Horan stopped him, pointing at his ravished door. Paul Martiny could think fast and did so. He said in a whisper:

'So soon?'

Horan nodded.

Paul Martiny had realized the situation but that didn't help him to make a decision. He had noticed the gun and he hated the sight of it. Michael Horan unarmed was alarming enough: with a firearm he was quite simply terrifying. His skin was as taut as a drumhead, his lips were white. That wouldn't be in fear, Paul thought. Horan had lost control again, he was fused for some action he'd never escape from. Paul said in an even lower whisper:

'I should put that thing away.'

No answer.

'Then I'll go in first.'

'You're not coming at all.'

Paul's answer to this was to push the door open but Michael beat him to the actual entry. He was holding the gun two-handed in front of him.

Two men got up from the sofa together. Crophead put a hand in his pocket and Horan's trigger finger tightened. Paul made a sideways grab and missed. The shot went away with a firm clear crack and a vase on the mantelshelf echoed the sound as it disintegrated into a dozen pieces. Crophead stayed standing, stiff and still. Horan pointed again but the smooth young man saved him. He said in his rather casual voice:

'All firearms are a sort of stalemate.'

The words were so utterly unexpected that they checked Michael Horan as no threat would have calmed him. This exquisite, Paul Martiny decided, can hardly be an honest man, working as he does for Lucas and calling with an obvious hoodlum, but it's certain that he's no kind of coward.

The young man turned to Paul Martiny, smiling politely in recognition of a second sane and sensible man. 'Shall we sit down?' he suggested. He did so. Paul followed him and then Mike Horan. Crophead hesitated but finally joined him. Michael still held the pistol on Crophead but the tension had notably lowered.

The young man proceeded to lower it further. 'I was saying that all pistols are stalemate.' He might have been at a cocktail party. 'I meant that any man who pulls one implies that he is prepared to use it. Which the man at whom he's pointing the thing knows perfectly well that he will not do. In most cases, that is. Not here.' He nodded at Horan but stayed looking at Paul. 'For your friend did fire and he happily missed. So "stalemate", perhaps, was an ill-chosen word.'

Paul Martiny was ready to play this game. Get the temperature down, decrease it quickly. He said in his most conversational tone:

'I'd have fired myself.'

'I venture to doubt it.'

'I would if I'd been attacked.'

'But you weren't.'

They turned their heads to look at the other two, moving them in unison, synchronized. Crophead had his mouth open, lost. Mike Horan was still holding the pistol but his air of desperate anger was fading. Paul Martiny said, still matter-of-factly:

'If it isn't an impertinence I shouldn't have thought this was quite your cup.'

'How right you are—it normally isn't. What happened is that my friend over there is sometimes inclined to exceed his instructions. If I had to use jargon I greatly mistrust I should say he was a bit of a sadist. So his orders were to do his stuff and that stuff would have been very painful for *your* friend. But he wasn't to go beyond simple mayhem and our master knows very well that he likes to. So I was sent to keep the affair within limits.'

'And could you have done so?' Paul Martiny was curious.

'Certainly,' the young man said. One moment he sat there empty-handed, the next he was holding a pistol, laughing. 'Forgive me the melodramatic gesture. In fact I greatly mistrust these things and men who carry them even more.' He looked reflectively at Michael Horan. 'A great pity your friend cannot pay his debt.'

'But he can pay his debt and I told him to do so.'

'Forgive me an unseemly question. But is that the truth? I have got to know.'

'Of course it's the truth—I've no motive to lie to you.' The two civilized men had taken over, ignoring the others: they might not have been there. 'When

178

Horan was summoned to see Mr Lucas he had a cheque in his pocket to clear the whole matter. If Lucas hadn't bullied him, if Lucas had acted with moderation, he'd have paid and you wouldn't be here today.'

The young man asked quietly: 'Your cheque?'

'It was not but I can guarantee it.'

'Is it still valid?'

'It surely is.'

The young man stroked his chin uncertainly. 'My instructions were to limit the violence. I've no others which cover this new development, and Lucas is not a man to approve when his servants do something he hasn't told them.'

'Such as having a drink?'

'That's extremely kind.'

Paul Martiny rose and poured two gins. He might have been at home and behaved like it. He had forgotten Michael Horan completely and Crophead he had assessed correctly. In a situation which he understood he'd behave with an outrageous brutality but in one which was wholly new to him he would sit there breathing hard and muttering.

Paul brought the drink. 'May I make a suggestion?'

'I'd be something more than grateful to hear it.'

'If I were in your place I'd feel free to refer—back to Lucas, I mean, and risk his anger. After all the position has changed entirely. First my kinsman is armed and he's shown that he'll use it. That may not interest Lucas himself but it will interest your hairless friend in that chair or anyone else of his nasty profession whom Lucas may choose to send out again. What will interest Lucas is much more tempting.

179

The man you came to assault can pay.'

'Will you make yourself responsible?'

'Yes.' It came out with an extreme of reluctance. It was the final involvement. Martiny hated it.

Horan said suddenly: 'No.'

'Be quiet.' Martiny and the smooth young man had spoken the words together, sharply.

The telephone rang and Martiny went to it. He listened and then said: 'Thank you. I'll tell him.' He returned to the smooth young man and sat down again. 'The suggestion I made I still think sound—to refer back to Lucas for further instructions. Unhappily you cannot do so.'

'A further development?'

'Yes indeed. That message was for you.'

'And it said?'

'It said that Rex Lucas is dead. Shot dead.'

Enzo in a successful career had taken many men's lives for profit but he had only killed once in his life in anger. It wasn't a thing a professional did and, sitting in his taxi to Lucas, he was anxious to reassure himself that his motives weren't those of a vulgar revenge. This he succeeded in doing quite easily. He wasn't ignorant of his nation's history, particularly of the Roman Empire, and Byzantium had been part of that. Where Greeks had been the servants, often slaves. Their undoubted intelligence had sometimes been useful till they tried to overreach their masters, who then threw them to the fishes where they belonged. There was no substitute for military power as the British had in turn discovered. Their own empire was crumbling under their feet so they

180

had tried to control American policy by whispering in American ears. And it had worked for a year or two, they'd been clever. Like some stoned Greek slave with his master's ear, impotent but subtle and cunning. He'd believed he had had his hands on the levers, the controls of the enormous power which this semi-barbarian race had created. And he hadn't, he'd had nothing at all. When it had come to the realities —discipline, who could best use real power—this privileged, often pampered Greek eunuch had been fortunate to die swiftly and cleanly. Enzo released a sigh of contentment. He wasn't killing for any personal motive, he was doing as his ancestors would have, punishing an impertinent servant; he was doing no more than a Roman's duty.

He paid off the taxi at Rex Lucas's door, climbing the impressive steps down which Mike Horan had been brutally kicked, ringing the bell and waiting confidently. He had good reason to be quietly confident since his plan, like all good ones, was utterly simple. He was prepared that someone other than Lucas might recognize him and know his name, but he'd been alone with Rex Lucas when he'd talked of departure and told him the time of his flight out of England. That was still scheduled for half past one with the check-in time at one o'clock. He looked at his watch: it was five past noon. Fifty-five minutes to do what he must, then take a taxi to Heathrow in comfort. It was possible Lucas had given orders that he wasn't to be received or admitted, in which case men other than Lucas himself might get injured or if they persisted killed; or someone might hear his silenced gun, and in that case the same thing stood to happen. Enzo hoped sincerely for neither. He was a professional killer who loathed casual violence. Inescapably it was always undignified.

But nothing whatever untoward happened, for Lucas had been wrongly convinced that when Enzo spoke of return he was bluffing. He had therefore given no orders concerning him, certainly no instructions to bar him. The man who answered his ring had never seen him. Crophead and the smooth young man were engaged at this moment in Horan's flat and Pigs' Eyes was having his weekly day off. So the manservant who opened to him did so politely and asked him to wait. He then rang up to Lucas's office, who was faced with an instant and awkward decision.

It didn't take him long to make it. The absence of his regular hoodlums had deprived him of his standing protection and the manservant wasn't qualified in any sort of mayhem or violence. Even if Lucas told him to try it the result would be to infuriate Enzo, make him angrier than no doubt he was, and the odds against any success were enormous. Lucas sighed but he knew when his luck had broken. He went to his wall safe and counted a thousand; he put the notes on the desk with another sigh. Then he telephoned down to the door.

'Show him up.'

When Enzo came in he dismissed the manservant. Enzo sat down without being asked to. If he noticed the notes on the desk he did not say so. He sat motionless in a total silence.

Lucas wasn't yet frightened, he saw no need to be. He was going to lose a thousand pounds, a matter which he greatly resented, but he hadn't an inkling he was losing his life. 'I'm delighted that you've called,' he said. 'I find there has been a mistake, as you said, and sending money abroad is always awkward.'

Enzo didn't reply to this.

Lucas looked at the money. 'You'll find that correct.'

'I haven't a doubt I should find it correct.'

'I'd rather you counted it just the same.'

Enzo's answer to this was to reach to his shoulder. The weapon which came away with his hand was small but it was beautifully balanced. Deliberately, with an air of detachment, Enzo fitted it with an impressive silencer. While doing so he kept it on Lucas.

Rex Lucas went ceiling white. He said: 'Jesus.'

'If you wish to say a proper prayer I will give you a minute to make your peace.' Enzo was a devoted Catholic.

But Lucas didn't pray; he dropped his hand. He had a gun in a drawer of his desk; he never reached it. Enzo shot him in the forehead neatly, precisely where a Hindu woman wore the painted red spot of her married status.

He waited for perhaps two minutes, reassuring himself that the strangled clunk of the German and very efficient silencer had not been heard outside the room, then he picked up the money and went out quietly. He had made his recce, and knew his way, but in fact he saw no one. He opened the door.

He found a taxi at St George's Hospital and directed it to Heathrow airport. He checked in and his flight took off on time. He was travelling Alitalia, first class since he could well afford to, and the stewardess offered a glass of champagne. She offered it in excellent English for she'd mistaken him for an Englishman. Enzo wasn't offended, indeed he was pleased. He knew that his air of casual distinction was something which was very English, and if the sort of Englishman who wore it like an old school tie was also often extremely stupid, that wasn't a matter which troubled Enzo. He had never doubted his own intelligence.

So he answered the girl in his own good English, but he declined the champagne for gin and tonic. He liked champagne upon proper occasions but didn't consider that this was one of them. He had nothing to celebrate, nothing to toast. He'd enjoyed no good fortune, achieved no triumph. He had merely discharged an evident duty.

In Mike Horan's flat there was total silence. Crophead's jaw had fallen further, the other three men were thinking hard. For each this death of a man none liked, Rex Lucas whom someone had shot like a dog, had a different and sometimes propitious message. The smooth young man broke the silence at last, looking at Michael Horan now.

'There wasn't any firm or company, Rex Lucas was a one-man band. You're a very lucky man indeed.' He then turned to Crophead with open contempt. It was clearly a relief to show it. 'You,' he said curtly, 'are out of a job and so are several others like you. That goes for me too.' He returned to Martiny. His manner had changed from contempt to irony. 'I was a competent accountant once. I suppose you couldn't use one. No?'

18

The possession of a substantial fortune in a safe and very discreet Dutch bank had made surprisingly little difference to the way Mike Horan lived and thought. He had bought himself a better piano, a Georgian desk which he'd always envied and a modest but efficient car. He knew that he need never work and for the moment was content to idle, but later he'd find himself something interesting. Not counter-industrial espionage again, he'd had that once and the work had betrayed him, and it wouldn't be the City. He loathed it. Above all things it wouldn't be anything amateur, one of those jobs in Social Service where the almost audible capital letters concealed very poor pay and no prospects whatever. A shop, perhaps, not too far from London, a grocer's shop in some pleasant small town. The multiples would undercut him, he'd never grow rich and he didn't now need to, but people still used their local shops and Michael liked meeting all kinds of men. One day maybe a girl would come in, not grand and certainly not a Charlotte, but sensible and firmly tolerant, one who could ride his wicked temper.

And thinking of Charlotte he had done the right thing, not by Charlotte or her monstrous mother but by Melsome whom they'd cruelly entangled. Michael Horan didn't much fancy Melsome and his patronage had been hard to take, but behind it had been a solid principle which he'd had to acknowledge and much respected. Melsome was pompous, put other men's backs up, but when fortune smiled he would share her favours and he'd come first to a kinsman who'd once been in jail. So Michael had given Clement his freedom, the twenty-two thousand pounds he'd owed Lucas. If Lucas hadn't behaved with stupidity Mike Horan would have paid his debt, and debt it remained though Lucas was dead. What more satisfying way to discharge it than to give it to Melsome and set him free? The man had very obvious faults but Mike hadn't a reason to think him stupid. It was certain he hadn't a taste for suicide and Mike didn't believe he would marry Charlotte, lumber himself with her mother as mother-in-law, if he possessed a modest but useful fortune which he owed in no way whatever to either. He must have seen through them both by now so good luck to him.

Paul Martiny had arranged it all, using his cousin Kenneth, the banker. The letter Leigh had sent Clement Melsome had been impressive in its stilted simplicity. If Mr Melsome would be kind enough to call on the undersigned in London he would hear something to his great advantage.

So Clement had gone up to London, excited but also completely mystified. It couldn't be Lilian Gregg's estate, he knew by now that was five thousand pounds, rather less when they'd paid her debts and buried her. Her bank statements had disclosed the fact that a year or two before her death she'd drawn an enormous cheque to a jeweller and the jeweller had confirmed the transaction. But of the diamonds he'd sold her there wasn't a trace. There'd been a frantic search in the manor's ruins but the diamonds, if they'd ever been there, had been carted away in lorries of rubble, or perhaps some fortunate building worker had found them and was sitting pretty. Another even more febrile search in the villa where aunt Lilian had moved. This had yielded a little more, a hidey-hole. But that had been disappointingly empty. There hadn't been a trace of insurance.

Clement Melsome had realized he'd slipped from favour. Charlotte Tellier had been treating him distantly, Dorothy had been simply rude. He wasn't now a desirable bachelor, he was a clergyman with under five thousand pounds.

He arrived at Edlers very excited and was shown to Leigh's room with a certain ceremony. Kenneth Leigh had made his own researches for he hated what he called blind dates, and he knew most things about the Reverend Clement including (this from his cousin Martiny) that a woman intended to marry him for money which an unscrupulous mother had obtained, or rather had failed to obtain, from Lilian Gregg by debatable methods. And Lilian Gregg was the banker's kinswoman as also she was Paul Martiny's.

He received Clement Melsome with formal courtesy.... It was very kind indeed to have called. A stranger might have thought from Leigh's manner that Melsome was doing him some great favour, cutting him in on a deal worth millions, and in fact he didn't dislike Melsome. He had heard he was a screaming pouf but he was a High Churchman himself and coolly tolerant. In any case most country parsons were people he admired and respected, and when it came to brute business they were surprisingly shrewd. Some angel held his mantle around them. So he said when Melsome had drunk his first sherry:

'There are twenty-two thousand pounds in this bank. They are held to your account quite freely.'

Clement Melsome stared, then he asked inevitably:

'Where do they come from?'

'I can't tell you that.'

'It sounds very unusual, it makes me wonder. Is this a gift I can honourably accept?'

If the banker thought the adverb pompous he didn't show a sign of his feeling. 'I know its source but I may not disclose it. But I would not suggest you do anything wrong.'

'You assure me of that?'

'I assure you solemnly.'

Melsome began to make noises: Leigh stopped him. 'If you're thinking of the tax position it is one which I have considered myself. Unless you wish to leave it here as money earning no interest whatever it will have to be invested wisely, and of course you will have to report the income to whichever Inspector deals with your business.'

'But suppose he wants to know where it came from?'

Leigh nodded in appreciation: his judgement had been right again. This man wasn't a fool when it came to realities. 'We have excellent accountants here and a certain name in the world of banking. Assuming, of course, that you wish to use us.'

'By all means. I'd be very grateful.'

'That's really very kind again.' To Edlers twenty-two thousand pounds was chickenfeed for indifferent hens but Kenneth Leigh contrived to convey that the account would do him a personal favour. In fact it would be an unwelcome nuisance but he was accepting it to oblige Paul Martiny. Blood was thicker than water and always would be. 'That leaves the question of how to invest it. Have you any particular fancies?'

'I'm ignorant.'

'Rather less than you make out, I suspect. So you'll know that with interest rates as they are the sum you have, invested for income, will give you at least two thousand gross. Of course if you invest it like that you'll have no hedge against an increasing inflation, but I gather you needn't consider a family.'

It was a fly to the fish and Clement rose to it. 'I'm engaged,' he said but he didn't speak joyfully.

'Ah yes. Of course.' It was spoken quite neutrally. 'Then for the moment we'll invest as you say and later, if your circumstances change, we can consider the need to protect the capital. Not that equities nowadays are much protection when a so-called constitutional party talks openly of sequestration.' Kenneth Leigh rose and shook hands politely. 'We're agreed then?'

'Yes, thank you.'

'Then I'll have it attended to.'

As they walked across the splendid carpet the banker's manner subtly changed. So far he'd been polite and businesslike, talking to a prospective customer. Now he spoke with the authority of a great position and longer years.

'You will forgive an older man if he's frank?'

'In your case very gladly indeed.'

'Then you now possess a modest fortune, not a great one by modern standards but solid. There are people who'll seek to take advantage, and I don't mean men who will call at your rectory calling themselves investment brokers.'

'I understand you,' Clement Melsome said.

And in fact he had understood very well, but sitting in his shabby study, in the chair which Charlotte had once decided should be one of the first things to go, he didn't quite know what to do. He doubted. Charlotte and Mrs Dorothy Tellier were arriving for lunch at their own invitation and he knew what they were going to do. They would put him to the Question ruthlessly.... What, then, had happened, what had gone wrong? Where was the rest of the money, her jewellery? What was he, as executor, going to do? The Will wasn't being challenged. What now?

And he wasn't going to do a thing. That decision had been simple to take but it wouldn't be easy to face it out with a woman like Mrs Dorothy Tellier. He frowned since for once he was honestly angry. With Charlotte alone he'd have stood his ground, but to bring that awful mother.... Unfair.

... Unfair, but was he being the same? Charlotte probably wouldn't marry him if she thought he had some five thousand pounds, but he didn't have five he had twenty-seven. Did he owe it to Charlotte to tell her this?

This time he didn't seek guidance in prayer but considered it as matter of business. If he told Charlotte Tellier he was now passing rich there'd be a lifetime of these lunches together, exacerbated from time to time by a mother-in-law he now detested. And if he didn't elect to tell her his news she would probably break off their engagement. No doubt there was a very slim chance that she'd stick to him for better or worse and that would create a new situation. Then he'd be morally bound to marry her and then they would have entrapped him for ever. But it was perfectly fair, indeed it was wisdom, to put her to a simple test. He had a right to do that; he was going to exact it.

He rose from his chair in his spotted cassock to talk to the woman who cooked his lunch. For once he was brief and surprisingly succinct. Kenneth Leigh's angel spoke lucidly for him.

'I've been called to the other parish urgently. Please give my guests lunch and make my apologies.'

He slipped out at the back and walked down a field path. There was an interesting boy in his second parish and Clement was preparing him. For Confirmation, of course. That went without saying.

When he returned his lunch was uneaten. On his study table he saw a ring. It had cost him what at the time he had bought it was more than he could well afford. Now he picked it up and looked at it curiously. Then he threw it in the study fire.

He went into his dressing-room smiling, and there he washed his hands meticulously.

Michael Horan had spent a long weekend at Paul Martiny's house in the country. They had walked round the farms and shot a pheasant. Since it was out of season this act was illegal, but the bird had been an old cock, a nuisance. They had also eaten simply but well and Matty had been very charming.

She had also been extremely surprised, for Matilda Martiny had worked it out wrongly. She knew much more of her husband's safety valve, the criminals whose affairs he managed, then she would ever venture to tell him openly—the wise woman could hold her tongue in peace—and it had never been Paul Martiny's custom to ask them to stay in his house as guests. So she'd assumed that this man was a special exception and had behaved as she felt a hostess must. Moreover she had approved of Mike Horan. For a criminal he had excellent manners.

Now they were seeing him off at the door as he climbed into his little car. 'Thank you and goodbye,' Mike said.

'A pleasant journey and *au revoir*.'

Man and wife walked back to the simple porch. Paul Martiny hadn't meant *'au revoir'*. He'd had more than a fellow feeling for Horan and he'd helped as he'd decided he must. But he didn't wish to see him again. Such men were altogether too dangerous.

As he opened the door for his wife he said:

'Thank you for being so nice. That's that.'

Placid Matty who had it all wrong said comfortably:

'Till the next time, dear. But don't take risks.'